Amanda O'Callaghan is a Brisbane-based author whose short stories and flash fiction have been published and won awards in Australia, the United Kingdom and Ireland. Her work has been awarded and shortlisted in the Bath Flash Fiction Award, Flash 500, Carmel Bird Award, Aeon Award, Bristol Short Story Prize and Fish Short Story Prize. A former advertising executive, Amanda holds English degrees from King's College London, and a PhD from the University of Queensland. In 2016 she was a recipient of a Queensland Writers Fellowship. *This Taste for Silence* is her debut collection and was shortlisted for the Readings New Australian Fiction Prize. www.amandaocallaghan.com

THIS TASTE
FOR SILENCE

AMANDA O'CALLAGHAN

UQP

First published 2019 by University of Queensland Press
PO Box 6042, St Lucia, Queensland 4067 Australia
Reprinted 2019

uqp.com.au
uqp@uqp.uq.edu.au

Cover design by Josh Durham, Design by Committee
Author photograph by Peter Taylor, Shotglass Photography
Typeset in Bembo Std 11/15pt by Post Pre-press Group, Brisbane
Printed in Australia by McPherson's Printing Group

  Queensland This project is supported by the Queensland
Government Government through Arts Queensland.

 The University of Queensland Press is
assisted by the Australian Government
through the Australia Council, its arts
funding and advisory body.

ISBN 978 0 7022 6037 7 (pbk)
ISBN 978 0 7022 6201 2 (pdf)
ISBN 978 0 7022 6202 9 (epub)
ISBN 978 0 7022 6203 6 (kindle)

 A catalogue record for this
book is available from the
National Library of Australia

To Ade and Louis

Contents

A Widow's Snow

Roger, Maureen decided, is the kind of man who would appreciate an old-fashioned pudding. She flicked through the best of her recipe books, toyed with ideas like spiced apple tart with a rich pastry crust – Gerald's favourite, so not really an option – and all manner of sponges, even soufflés. She braved the mole-eyed newsagent (twice divorced, blinking at the door for a new, early rising wife) and bought a couple of cookery magazines. The desserts there, lashed down by guy ropes of toffee, subdued under heavy drifts of icing sugar, still seemed to totter on their plates. One wobbly chocolate affair, stacked high and leaning, put her in mind of the ramshackle house on the Scottish coast where she and Gerald had gone on their honeymoon. She remembered lying in his arms for the first time, naked and happy in the cavernous room, wondering whether the whole creaking place might, with one more movement, tip into the howling sea.

By the end of the week, she'd discounted them all. Too insubstantial. She'd seen how Roger conducted his business. 'No, not the sort of thing I'm interested in, thank you,' he'd say, dropping the phone back into its cradle with a decisive clunk. There was a certainty about everything he did. Maureen envied that. Now that she was cooking for him for the first time, she didn't want the merest touch of a dessert fork dismantling the whole effect. She wanted something that kept its shape, something robust. Later on, she'd make one of those fragile confections. Not for this dinner.

She stirred the batter. The scent of the mixed spices curled around her, reaching languidly across the oak table and into the corners of the warm room. It was a long time since she'd made fig pudding. She'd forgotten its festive perfume. Just a week into the new year, the kitchen shelves still edged with ivy, it seemed an appropriate choice.

Looking out the window towards the neighbouring field, where a pony had been startled into cantering for no obvious reason, Maureen felt happier than she'd been in a long time. Contented, she corrected herself, as the large wooden spoon – once her mother's – turned the mixture.

The sky, which earlier had been choked with cloud, had all but cleared. It would freeze later, she knew. Guiding her small palette knife around the bowl, she garnered the last of the mixture. She scraped the batter from the spoon, running the knife down its bone-strong length until it was clean. Smoothing the hillocks of mixture, she laid discs of paper over the top and bound them in place with a craftswoman's nimble fingers.

'That should do nicely,' she said aloud. Since losing Gerald, she was not afraid to talk to herself, to hear her voice ring out in the empty rooms.

As she pushed the basin into the oven, her eye was drawn to the benchtop, where she saw that the roses in her new vase, the one Roger had given her, were beginning to droop. She must change them before tomorrow night.

The vase was nice, in its way, she thought.

'Rare, Maureen,' Roger had said, in the same voice he used with his customers. 'It's Spode. Pearlware. 1820. There's not many like it around. Certainly not in this condition.'

She repositioned the slumping flowers. Roger's vase was large and almost shockingly bright. It had a lapis blue background with broad green leaves entwined all over it. Here and there, an oriental eye of neon pink flower blinked through the foliage. Every leaf on the vase was yellowed at the tip, as if the pattern itself was at some kind of turning point, the moment when ripeness begins to spoil, when beauty becomes a far-off thing. Those yellow edges bothered her.

It was a Christmas present. The first real gift from him, surprisingly generous. 'Now, Maureen, I want you to unwrap this very carefully,' he'd told her, setting it on the hall table. Before she could pull back the wrapping – she could see the colours flaring through the tissue – he blurted out, 'It's a vase,' like a child.

'It's a lovely shape,' she said to him, noticing the yellow-edged leaves, even then.

Roger told her about its provenance, but most of the detail washed over her. She knew nothing about porcelain. She did remember that he'd told her the vase was clobbered. She'd nodded at this as if she knew exactly what he was talking about. After he left, she checked the vase all over, believing it must be slightly damaged in some way. Later, when she admitted this to him, he laughed so hard he knocked over his wineglass.

'Oh, Maureen,' he said, patting her hand, oblivious to the pooling wine, 'you do cheer me up.'

While a waiter mopped at the spill, they ate small pyramids of cheese and shrivelled muscatels, and Roger explained the process of clobbering. As far as Maureen could work out, it meant one layer of decoration put over another. Overdecorated.

And that's what it is, she thought, as she leaned against her kitchen bench. Those snarling bright colours, those throttling leaves. She preferred muted tones. Gerald had never been one for anything too showy. 'It's just not our thing, is it, love?' he used to say.

The pale roses were refusing to rally under her hand. They drooped against the wide lip of Roger's vase, looking insipid. She regarded her clotted cream walls, the watery green plates stacked on an open shelf beside her. She wondered how someone, seeing this kitchen, this house, might describe its owner. She pulled the roses out in one swift movement and drove them all, headfirst, into the bin.

Perhaps, she thought, Roger never intended me to actually use the vase. This made the blood rush to her face. It still felt new, this life after Gerald, this confusing business of being alone. The glare of it, after so long in the pleasant shadow of married life. And now, this new world of dinners out, and makers' marks, and Roger Kempton with his knife-creased trousers, and his good cologne that smelled, not unpleasantly, of the old leather hymn books from school.

He's quite handsome, in a broad-faced way, she thought, wiping a tiny mound of spilled sugar into her cupped hand. She hadn't really noticed Roger's looks until the time he'd been delayed by a big sale. He'd come striding through the restaurant towards her, wearing a burgundy-coloured cashmere as thin as muslin. He always wore those cashmere pullovers. When the weather was particularly cold, he'd wear two, the polo neck beneath reaching almost to his jawline. Maureen wondered whether it felt a little strangling, all that close-knit wool.

Roger had good hair. Dark silver. He kept it cut very short as if he'd served as a soldier and couldn't quite shake off military strictures. Perhaps he *had*, she thought, amazed to realise that, months on, she knew very little about his background. Why hadn't she asked?

There'd been a woman, a while back. He'd mentioned her in passing. 'A good few years,' he told her, when she asked how long they were together. 'But that was a thousand years ago,' he said, then changed the subject.

The scent of the pudding was rising around her. Maureen

caught sight of her profile reflected in the kitchen window. She drew back her wide shoulders into a better posture, put her hands on her hips, watched her breasts rise in the glass. She felt an unexpected longing for the shapely waist that had once been hers.

She could see the outline of her hair, brushed into a soft helmet. The dark hanks that had once swooped heavily across her back were long gone. Stop being ridiculous, Maureen thought. A thousand years ago, indeed.

Outside, the sky had turned a pale, flawless blue. Unaccountably, she shivered in the yeasty warmth.

He brought flowers. Deep purple peonies, their petals drawing back from the centre, leaving a creamy cavity open like a surprised mouth.

'They say this is the last of it,' he said, brushing epaulettes of snow from the shoulders of his coat.

It had snowed for most of the previous night, and billows had pushed against the kitchen window all day as Maureen cooked. As she closed the hall door, she noticed high mounds forming on either side of the path.

'They're beautiful,' she said, taking the flowers, feeling a sudden gush of shyness. 'I'll put them in water straight away, before we sit down.'

'Not in the Spode, I hope,' he called after her, and his too-loud voice seemed to bounce down the hall behind her.

Maureen felt a singe of heat in her cheeks. She did not turn. 'No,' she said. 'Of course not.'

She heard Roger stamp the snow from his boots onto the flagstones. He followed her in.

Maureen had always thought the sitting room was beautiful, but now she wasn't so sure. The expensive furniture she'd bought from Hempsey's had begun, tonight, to look a little plain. The small drinks table that Gerald had made after he retired seemed rather gauche and unfinished. She was thankful for the few nice pieces of inherited crystal on the bureau. Roger's eyes had settled on them with an approving, if brief, glance.

His vase looked garish beside the crystal, but it was jolly and bright, and he was gratified to see it there, she felt sure. He would have found the rest of the room colourless, she imagined, as she watched him raise the brandy glass to his lips and stretch his legs towards the fire.

She hadn't been to his house yet. She looked forward to seeing what it was like, which pieces he prized enough to bring into his own home. She'd wondered about it. But so far she'd always met him at his shop. She didn't even know where he lived, beyond the fact that it was a few miles out on the other side of town.

She liked calling in to the shop. She'd sit on the floral slipper chair in the corner while Roger served his customers. She'd try to make herself inconspicuous by leafing through books on Edwardian glassware, or that great thick folder with pictures of spoons, nothing else. She'd imagine the families who once sipped and ate from these things. She'd think of the homecomings, the grand dinners. All the clink and clatter across the decades. She'd think, too, of the empty places: the sons lost at war, the daughters lost in childbirth. It made her feel, as antiques always did, a little sad.

She liked hearing Roger discuss a piece of china or silver that had taken someone's eye. Antiques did not make him sad; their beauty energised him. His big voice always seemed out of keeping with whatever delicate piece he might be handling: the miniature cruet set; that arching spoon in heavy silver; the tiny pink teapot in the window. 'It's French, Maureen. Limoges. Lovely piece.' She liked his commanding presence. Others did, too. The business did well.

But tonight, Roger spoke rather quietly as they sat in her matching, string-coloured armchairs. The dinner had been a triumph. Stilton soup, roast beef in a light jus – he'd had two servings – and the fig pudding, perfect and scented, imported raspberries skirting the edges, a buttery clot of cream sliding in the warmth. A rich, wintry meal. Delicious, if she did say so herself.

Perhaps this is the beginning of something, Maureen thought, as she watched him relax. Not a friendship. Since meeting him at the shop, she felt they'd been friends, although the thought of what happened that first day still made her cringe. She'd been cleaning out cupboards all morning. In the hallway, she'd stacked a little cairn of Gerald's old things, which she planned to throw away.

She felt a jolt of guilt every time she looked at them, but relief, too. Stopping for lunch, she'd taken down the stack of painted dessert plates that were kept in a glass-fronted cabinet. On a whim, she'd wrapped them in a cloth, put them in a flat-bottomed basket, carried them into the village and up the narrow footpath to Kempton Antiques.

She didn't know why she did this. To get them valued? To sell them? The plates had been in Gerald's family for years. They'd only been used for special occasions, then carefully handwashed and stacked away. Before Gerald had inherited them, they'd taken pride of place in what had been known to generations of his family as 'the good cupboard'.

The basket was cumbersome. She'd spotted Roger through the shop window, sitting at a broad, carved desk. He glanced up at her approach. 'Come in, please,' he called to her. He had not risen from his chair, but his face was friendly.

Maureen set the basket on the desk without a word, unwrapped the plates with nervous hands. 'We've had these a long time,' she said, offering no further detail, finding herself overcome with emotion.

Roger gave her a small, encouraging nod. He looked at her for a few seconds before taking up one of the plates, turning it over, turning it back, putting it down. His eyes narrowed into a hard, appraising stare. Then he told her in a kind but firm voice that they were very pretty plates but of no commercial value whatsoever.

She'd stood for a moment, staring down at the stack of floral china, feeling a slight sway, wondering, stupidly, if the floor was giving way. Then she burst into great hiccuping sobs.

Roger could not have been more considerate. He guided her to the slipper chair, where she cried into a series of tissues from a box that he'd placed at her elbow. She tried to compose herself, but when she thought of the long years of reverence for those worthless plates, her life with Gerald also seemed to become something trivial, even bogus.

Roger made her tea in the small kitchen at the back of the shop and brought it to her on a dainty oval tray. 'Take your time,' he said. 'It's quiet today. Too sunny for antique lovers.'

Maureen had seen people stretched in the sun beside the river as she'd walked into town. Lying prone on the bare grass, they looked like they'd been washed up in a flood.

After her tears subsided, they talked a little. As if to soothe her, he showed her things in the shop he thought particularly beautiful.

'This is Belleek,' he said, holding up a large basket-weave bowl, each creamy strand spaghetti thin and perfect. 'Parian china. From Northern Ireland. Black stamp,' he'd added, almost in a whisper. 'There's nothing,' he said, shaking his head like a doting father, 'that could possibly upset the perfection of this piece.'

Maureen had become used to this sort of fervour in the time since.

And now, as she watched Roger lounge before the fire, things seemed different. She was comfortable, that was it. She hadn't felt like this for a long time. Since Gerald. Tonight, she didn't feel that aching sense of being uncoupled, the scratch and prickle of eyes judging and pitying. Here in this room, with Roger, she didn't mind being a widow.

She worried the room was too hot.

'I grew up in South Africa,' he said. 'The hotter the better.'

She'd thought he was English. She found herself listening for the small rasp of accent. It was there. So obvious, now that she knew.

She asked about his family. His father had been an engineer, he told her. A looming, sunburned presence who disappeared into the bush for long periods, building roads and bridges. He had not approved of antiques.

'Dead people's stuff,' Roger said. 'That's what he used to call it. He's dead now, himself, of course. Ten years, I think.'

Something of a relief, Maureen thought. 'And your mother?' she asked.

'She's been gone a long time,' he said. 'Killed in a car accident when I was still at boarding school.' Maureen was about to speak when he added, 'She had an eye for beautiful things. Knew quite a lot about antiques, actually. And before you ask,' he said, irritation rising in his voice, 'I also have a sister in Germany, but she's rather strange. We don't have much contact.'

'I'm sorry.'

'Don't be,' he said, kindly enough. 'Anyway, that really was a magnificent meal.'

Although there was no question of it as far as Maureen was concerned, she was shocked to find she kept thinking about sex. Well, not sex, precisely. Nothing that involved her baring herself to him, perish the thought. Just odd flashes of something wonderful: bodies, warmth, happiness. She realised that it was a long time since anyone had touched her. Even a hug. The thought of this, and the tumbling images in her brain, flustered her. Her hands rose and fell in nervous movements. Four years, she thought. Gerald's been dead for over four years.

They'd had no children. A quiet kind of loss, like a sadness gone missing. One they never discussed in any deep sense. 'It's an awful shame, Maureen,' Gerald had said, when they knew for sure. 'Such a pity.' He had hugged her that day, and she'd felt his body galvanise in a great, dry sob before he strode out to the car without another word, leaving her staring into the swirling grain of the kitchen table. They rarely mentioned it again, but the absence of a child sometimes sat between them, solid and immovable.

'It's pretty amazing, Maureen. I've had a few brilliant finds there. There was that time I ...'

Roger was enthusing about a flea market in Lyon. Or was it Dijon? Maureen wanted him to stop. She wanted to talk about herself now. Tell him everything. Tell him about that moment when she'd traced the lines in the oak with her finger, and listened to the thrum of the tap dripping into the kitchen sink, wondering what rhythm could exist in a life, in a marriage, without a child at its heart.

'Coffee?' she said.

In the kitchen, she ran her hands under the cold tap, letting the water flow across her wrists, numbing them almost instantly. She was glad she'd kept the fire up so high: it was cold enough to freeze the pipes. On impulse, she rolled up the window blind. Far from stopping in the early evening, it had been snowing heavily for hours. The dark hedgerow on one side of the garden stretched back into the night, iced with a thick slab of snow.

She took the tray into the sitting room. Roger was inspecting his vase, or the crystal, perhaps.

'You need to see something,' she said.

She pulled back the drapes. The snow had brightened the night. They could see cut-out shapes of trees and fences.

'Look at that!' he said, hands on hips. 'Gorgeous. Bet the roads are going to be bad.'

'They'll be impassable,' she said. 'That's the heaviest snow I've seen for years.' She paused, feeling a little embarrassed. 'But you're welcome to stay. I have a spare room.'

Roger plucked at his cashmered neck. 'Oh, thank you,' he said. 'Looks like we'll be having breakfast together as well.'

They both smiled. It was going to be fine.

'Come on,' he said. 'How about another brandy with that coffee?'

It was over. Maureen sat, poised on the edge of the armchair, as if she meant to stand up at any moment. She pressed the remote; the television blinked on. Four dead in the Pennines. A whole family gone, their little dog miraculously alive. What came over some people, she thought, setting out like that? Dying, unnoticed, in their snow-white car. The news returned to London. Even there, amidst the concrete and asphalt, bodies were being found. It was a tragic turn of events, as Gerald would have said.

The snow had stopped at last, and the light was strong for late morning. She could see the sun pushing through the crack where the curtains stood slightly apart. Soon, there would be no snow outside, only grey-brown slush and icy floodwaters, and the spaces in the world where those frozen souls had been.

'You must come and have dinner at my place,' Roger had said.

This was late on the second night, the weather still too severe to leave. It had been a wonderful, unexpected time, cocooned in the house together. Leftovers for lunch, chess, some music. All very light-hearted. Innocent, really, she thought.

The snow amazed them.

'We're no better than children,' she said, as they stood together at the kitchen window, pointing out a heavy drift

14

caught in a roofline, icicles hanging from the eaves. Earlier that evening, she'd spotted her neighbour looking down on them. Maureen had waved up to her, feeling oddly proud. Her neighbour lifted her hand in half-salute and stepped back into the shadows.

Maureen cooked another dinner, smiling to herself at the strange twist of it all. The food was nothing grand this time, but still good. They ate in the kitchen – Roger had insisted – chatting across the oak table. They went back to the comfortable chairs for more brandy.

This second night seemed more open to possibilities. The fleeting images of bodies locked together – strangers' bodies – had gone from Maureen's thoughts, much to her relief. It was not impossible that they might share a bed tonight. The idea gave her a surge of happiness as well as terror.

She'd not spoken much about herself in the end. The need to confide in Roger had surprised her. She realised how lonely she'd been. She did say a little: how her family came from Scotland, her sister in the Philharmonic, even Gerald.

'How long were you married?' Roger asked. Just the one question. And his wordless nod at her answer seemed to shrink the forty-six years to something less substantial.

'A long time to be with the same person, isn't it?' she said, hating the defensive tremble in her voice.

'Unimaginable,' he replied. And she'd heard the accent then, clearer than ever before.

It was easier to talk about Roger.

'Did you always like antiques?' she asked him.

'No.' He hesitated, working his mouth as if it held a toffee. 'That came later.'

Maureen's balance seemed to be deserting her, even while sitting. The whisky before dinner, the wine, the brandy; there was a crowded tray of used glasses in the kitchen. She could see that Roger, who'd had much more, was feeling it, too.

'I ran a factory, once,' he said, looking almost ready to giggle, his eyes crinkling at the edges. 'An unlikely candidate, I suppose you're thinking.'

She was.

'It wasn't exactly a pickle factory, Maureen,' he said, with a smile. 'It was in the days when my father was still trying to badger me into a career in engineering. Well, this was engineering of sorts. It was a glass factory. You know, shop fittings and so forth. We made amazing things: room dividers, pool fences, balconies. Once, we made a fantastic glass spa with sides like huge, green waves. All very high-end. Beautiful, in its own way, but hardly Lalique.'

Roger was smoothing his hair with the flat of his hand, remembering. 'I enjoyed running the place, to tell you the truth. It was very successful. For a while, at least. Kept my father off my back.'

'What made you leave it?' she said. 'Fell in love with antique dealing, I suppose.'

How light her heart felt when she said that. How

romantic it was to be here, snowed in with this man. When she thought back over the conversation, and she did for the rest of her life, she remembered the pause in his story at that point, how he looked over to the vase in the way an actor might look into the wings for a prompt.

'I didn't know much about antiques, except what I'd picked up from my mother,' he said. 'We had that same love of craftsmanship. There's a kind of order in it, I guess.'

A kind of order. She would think about this for a long time afterwards.

'So why did you all leave South Africa?' she said. 'Was it the political scene?' She saw his eyes narrow, the way they had at the shop when he'd looked at her dessert plates for that one brief moment.

'We didn't all leave,' he said. 'I was the only one who left, back then. It was nothing to do with politics. That stuff didn't … affect us much.' His shoulders rose in a minute shrug. 'My father made me leave.'

Roger drained the last of his brandy as if he might go. Remembering that he was trapped, at least until morning, he made an elaborate show of replacing his glass on its linen coaster.

'Your father was pretty authoritarian.' The brandy was making her blunt.

'He was.' Roger grimaced. 'But in this case he was right. When I got to England, I found the glass business was a closed shop, so that was out. I went into antiques because it was the only other thing I knew. Or half knew.'

'But why leave South Africa? You said the glass place was successful.'

'It was. But something happened.'

Maureen felt a slow wave of discomfort wash across the room towards her.

'Something happened and I had to leave,' he said. He poured himself another brandy from the bottle beside him, and looked straight at her.

And there it was: that same hard stare. The stare that said if there's going to be a future to all this, Maureen, with you coming to dinner in my house, and maybe more, you telling me about the slow drip of that tap as the life you expected paled into something more colourless, then you need to know this.

The drink had made him daring.

'I see,' she said. She would not have asked any more. She often thought about that.

And she somehow knew what was expected of her. 'Oh, how dreadful,' she could say. 'It's a harsh place, South Africa, I've heard.' Something like that, something bland and final to speak out loud so that together they could watch the words lift in the thickened air and vanish like smoke. Order returned.

'I got rid of someone,' he said.

She would remember, too, the way her mind, soft at the edges from the brandy that she would never drink again, spun through the possible meanings in 'got rid of' like a roulette wheel. Round and round, a dull clicking in her head.

'What do you mean?' she said, hot blood coursing inside her ears.

He saw she was waiting.

'One of the workers at the factory,' he said. 'Little squat fellow. Took to calling himself the shop steward. Had an opinion on every damn thing. He had this irritating way of coming up too close, stepping into your personal space.' Roger's hand moved up and down, miming the intrusion. 'Sometimes, when he was talking, I could feel his breath on my neck. I hated that. I should never have given him a job, but he was the second cousin or something of one of our suppliers. The usual carry-on: connections and favours. Anyway, about a year in, this guy started causing a lot of trouble in the place. It'd been good till then. Everyone was happy enough.'

Roger turned back towards the fire. 'It wasn't just me invested in that business. There were local businessmen involved – my father's mates, naturally. You've no idea of the complications.' His voice trailed off. 'Three years after I gave that man a job, he'd all but ruined me. It was just incredible. People were giving me grief night and day. We were going broke, that's the truth of it. And my father got wind of it. Said he was coming back to sort out my mess.' Roger shook his head. 'You know, he had a way of saying, "I'm pretty disappointed," that you could hardly believe.'

Maureen looked over at the peonies, standing with their dark-lipped mouths.

'It's a funny thing,' he said. 'People can smell trouble,

Maureen. Nobody wants to deal with a business that's at war with its staff. They run a mile.' Roger was gazing deep into the flames. 'He was winning, in the end, and he knew it. The orders were dropping off. It was pure sabotage. Even some of the older guys – been with me for years – were starting to take an interest in their goddamn rights. Everything, the whole damn thing, was going to come tumbling down.'

'So you got rid of him,' she said.

'I knew I had to do something but I didn't have a plan,' he said. 'I suppose you could say fate took over. You know how that can happen.'

'Tell me,' she said.

He shook his head. 'It doesn't matter. It was a long time ago. God, it was – it was forty years ago. Everything's ... well, it's different now. Okay! It's forgotten.' He took a noisy gulp of his brandy and set it down on the table. 'Forgotten.'

'I really need to know, Roger,' she said, and she felt as if she could wait forever, her feet planted in the oatmeal carpet. Wait for the fire to die out, for the ice to set hard in the pipes, for the snow, the dreadful, blanketing snow, to bury them here. He *would* tell her tonight.

He stood up. For one ghastly moment, she thought that he might attack her. She felt herself brace in the chair, knew she was utterly defenceless. But he moved closer to the fire, put one hand on the high stone mantelpiece.

'He'd broken his arm.' Roger paused, putting a hand to his forehead. 'God, I can't remember his name ... imagine that.' He shook his head. 'Anyway, this guy, he'd slipped on a bit of machine oil. A bad break. Couldn't do any work. Useless – even more useless than he normally was. But he still kept mouthing off, sneaking around among the workers, telling them to demand this, demand that. There was a strike planned. A strike!' He looked back at Maureen as if this news might be astonishing.

'I knew that would mean the end of the business,' he said. 'I just couldn't bear it, the thought of my father getting involved. All of it would be so … public. I knew he wouldn't spare me in any way.'

She watched Roger's long fingers gripping the edge of the mantelpiece as if he meant to pull it towards him like a drawer.

'I was out walking one day,' he said. 'I used to walk in the bush quite a bit. Birds. Used to photograph birds. So beautiful, some of their feathers: fantastic colours and patterns. You couldn't believe how perfect, Maureen. I've still got some at home. I can show you.' He paused. 'Anyway, I knew the bush around there very well. My father had owned that land for years. It was private. Strictly private …' The fire spat a tiny ember onto the tiles. 'I thought I'd spotted a bird. A flash of yellow and blue. Next thing I look up and there he is,' he said. 'On our land. It was the sling I'd seen, it was so brightly coloured. And when he saw me, he didn't turn away, he just walked right up to me as if he meant to say something, but he didn't speak. He just stood there, really close, staring. I said to him, "What are you doing on my property?" and he just smiled and said, "Walking, just like you." And then he made to push past me on the track. Rude. Just so rude. I had a tripod with me that day. It was leaning against a tree on the other side of me, and ...' He looked at Maureen.

'And you hit him?' she said. A word was jangling in her mind, crazy as a funhouse. *Clobbered.* Clobbered him – that's what you did. That's what it means.

'Look,' he said, 'it was done before I knew it. It was just ... everything came at once and my hand went around the tripod and there he was, up so damn close, and his filthy breath on my neck.' Roger's mouth was working again. 'I didn't set out to kill him.'

'But you did kill him.'

They stared at each other.

'What did you do then?' she said. 'After you killed that man.' She was horror-struck by a need to laugh aloud. Here, in her own sitting room, in the linen union chairs, talking of murder. A murderer leaning on the mantelpiece, his handsome face explaining it all. Preposterous.

'You know, it's what the Greeks used to do,' he said. There was a small note of defiance in his voice.

'Greeks?' She thought she'd misheard.

'The Ancient Greeks. Pushing out troublemakers. Driving them into exile. Sometimes ... yes, sometimes killing them, for the greater good.' His voice sounded thinner, higher. 'That's what they did. To restore things. That's ... what they did.'

'What did you do after you killed that man?' she said again.

Roger dropped his hand from the mantelpiece, stretched both arms like someone who'd driven a long way. 'When I was a kid, I played there all the time. And my sister. We found a couple of deep hollows in the ground. We never did find out what they were, exactly. Not caves. Not man-made, I think. They were almost like sinkholes. Very well camouflaged. We used to hide in them. Terrifying, as kids on your own. They seemed huge to us then.'

He turned to her now, his face a plain, tight mask. A finely wrought shell of a face. 'I knew I was close to one of the holes that day,' he said. 'So I just dragged him down the hill and rolled him in. It was astonishingly simple, if you must know. And they didn't find him for years. My sister rang to tell me. She'd seen something in the local paper – used to get them sent to her in Germany. Nothing else ever emerged. My father could be very ... proficient whenever things needed sorting. That's all I can tell you, Maureen. Truly. That's all there is. It was a long time ago. A million miles from here. It was just something that happened.'

She stood up. She didn't feel afraid, which surprised her. She stepped towards him, pushed the brass guard against the mouth of the fireplace with a metallic scrape, and turned towards the door.

'I'm going to bed now, Roger,' she said, her hand on the doorknob. She felt the colder air slip in from the hall, wind around her legs like a needy cat. 'I want you to leave

23

at first light. There's a garden spade on the porch. You can dig your way out if necessary.'

Roger sat down, pushed his elegant hands around the curve of the armrests. He did not raise his head.

'We won't be seeing each other again,' she said. She'd never spoken to anyone in such an icy, calm voice.

He nodded slowly, as if he were only just taking everything in.

She turned to go.

'Maureen,' he said, in a quiet voice. She was sure he was going to say that he was sorry, how much he regretted all this.

'What is it?' she said.

He looked straight at her and, in a low, chivalrous voice, he said, 'Would it be too much to ask, do you think, if I took back the vase?'

In her bedroom, Maureen turned the key. She felt the metal components drop into place, heard the satisfying click. The silk tassel that dangled from the key swung against the glossy door. Gerald was always a great man for locks. His father had been a locksmith. It wasn't that they were afraid; they were just careful people. Ready.

She took the tweed rug from the upholstered chair in the corner. She lay down, fully clothed, on the thick bedspread, smoothed the lavender checks across her body. She kept her eyes open, watching the snow-lit square of window, waiting for morning.

An Uncommon Occurrence

You'll wait. Everything will feel, will be, upside down. Above you, the shape of ordinary things will lodge in your mind for later. The line of boxy lights, running out of sight, each stark bulb masked by its own frosted casing. The smoke alarms like buttons on a placket of ceiling. Everything neat and controlled, bar a strange bloom high up in one corner.

'Mind, please,' you'll hear – the hospital porter, older than your father, deep-voiced, steering. 'Off we go, love,' he'll say, as you're trundled into the corridor. You will not find mint green a soothing colour.

In the lift, no one will speak. You'll be the only one averting your eyes. You'll smell rain on woollen sleeves, stale nicotine, a perfume too heavy for daytime. You'll see a moth trapped, backlit, dead. You'll notice the music. Muzak, to be precise. For a precious moment this will distract you; the way it is something, and yet not. Half-baked.

As the lift rises, airless already, curiosity will press down. But there will be no wad of bandage, no translucent tubes piping mysterious liquids. You'll feel an insane desire to apologise. Unable to stop yourself, you'll remove your hands from beneath the covers. They'll see nothing missing, nothing serious. They'll be bored before the doors open.

The doctor will be kind. 'A very common occurrence, I'm afraid.' You will wonder about the word 'procedure'. It will tumble in your mind for a long time. She'll tell you it is simple, quick. You will be a model patient.

At home, you'll observe life in miniature: ants in a crooked line, a tiny curl of flaking paint, beads of water on glass. You will feel yourself reeling like a giant in a shrunken world. Your lover will take on extra shifts. Your mother will hem 'after what's happened' to the edge of every sentence. There will be no questions.

The woman at the fruit shop will say you look pale. You'll astonish yourself by telling her why. 'Yes, I'm fine now,' you'll assure her. 'Very common. Yes. True.'

But then she'll take your arm and gently steer you outside, past wooden crates piled high with apples and pears. She'll look straight at you and say, 'I'm so very sorry for your loss.'

The scent of the fruit will be almost unbearable. And when you cry out, she will not move away.

The Turn

It's the turn that tells you. There you are, idly watching a man carrying a black bin bag, making his way down a lane. You know the bag's heavy – you see that – and you've got nothing better to do than just sit in the car and think that maybe he works in one of those restaurants, so the bag's full of slops, pulpy and unstable, a horror show if it splits open. Or maybe he's been cleaning out rubbish, sorting out his spare room or his study. He might live in those apartments stacked above the shops. But you decide that he doesn't look like the studying kind. Funny how you know these things based on nothing, from just a glance. He's got his back to you, so you can't see his face; no idea about hair or skin colour. He's wearing dark clothes and some sort of beanie, but that's all you could say. Maybe he's got an unusual walk. Maybe you're imagining it. He's not moving very fast with the weight of the bag, so he might be middle-aged, or older. You know he's not well, the way he carries his shoulders a fraction too high. Emphysema. Might be lung cancer. A sick old man taking out his rubbish. All these things go through your mind in a matter of seconds.

'What are you thinking about?' Jackie used to ask me all the time.

'Nothing,' I'd tell her. But truth is, you're always thinking of something, always noticing.

The guy's almost at the back of the lane now. The traffic's heavy enough. Not much business around. He's about to disappear, and you've lost interest.

But then he turns.

Still holding the bag clear of the ground, he stops, swivels his body back towards you. You see a flash of white-skinned neck. He looks straight at you, like he can see you, only he can't because you're sitting in the dark, waiting for the lights to change. But it's the turn that makes you look more closely. It's not like he's heard something scrabbling near the bins, or footsteps behind him. This is slow, deliberate. Like he's checking that no one's watching.

But you are.

'You're a gloomy sod, Robbie Quinn,' Jackie used to say.

She always called me by my full name. Coming from her, it never felt strange. Same with the way she called me a sod. There was no malice in it. She said it about a lot of people. 'A poor old sod was brought in this morning and you should have seen his leg ...' Jackie's sod was harmless, affectionate even, unless she told you to *sod off*. Then you'd know she was annoyed. She sounded most English when she said that – the little snap of her accent coming through. It used to make me smile.

And, no, I wasn't gloomy. Not then. Jackie always thought that having a quiet moment meant you were getting depressed. She didn't like to think about things too deeply. Some days all I wanted to do was just sit at the table, sip my coffee and stare out into the street for half an hour. But it bothered Jackie. She'd start shuffling papers, pushing in chairs. 'When's your shift start?' she'd say. 'Aren't you going to your mother's first?' 'That coffee'll be cold as charity by now.' She'd annoy me out of my thoughts and I'd get going again, saving my quiet time for when she was at the hospital.

I sit at the window a lot now. Everything stays where I leave it. The coffee goes as cold as charity, whatever that means. When I look into the street, I notice everything.

A crowd is a terrible thing. I know it's foolish to say so because mostly a crowd has a purpose: commuters, shoppers, that posse of media in my front yard. In a crowd, pretty well everyone has a place to be. But for me, even after all this time, it's different, unnerving. I look at every face, assess every shape and size. I get entangled in the impossible knot of all those lives: the way they walk, hold their heads; their voices as they pass. Once, near the old bus station, I heard a frantic call, 'Robbie, Robbie,' and the accent was English and I said to myself, *Don't turn around. She always said your full name. It's not her. It can't be her.*

But at the last minute, I did turn, and I saw a woman with her arms outstretched, and a black dog racing away trailing a glittery red lead. And when someone caught the lead as the dog shot past, bringing him up tight like a cartoon character, front paws pedalling the air, I burst into a crazy cackle. Too loud, too high. And everyone stared – some with frozen smiles from watching the dog – because I was a man laughing alone in a crowd. A man who didn't have a place to go.

They thought it was me in the beginning. Some of the papers, all of the cops. Can't say I blame them. *Routine procedure.* I heard that a lot.

Mostly, it was two cops. One was almost small enough to be a jockey, except he had huge hands. The other was about my size, normal enough, but there was something of the cowboy about him. He had a Clint Eastwood squint in one eye when he spoke, like he was looking into a mirage down a highway. If he'd been an accountant or a bus driver you wouldn't notice it. But a detective; it was almost comical. Once, after he'd been questioning me for a long time, I could see the squint forming, and I'd started to smile.

'Something funny, Mr Quinn?' he said, and that eye shrank even more.

The jockey never said much, just watched, hunched over the table, those big hands all knotted up in front of him. Late one night, when Clint had his face up close and I was feeling light-headed, I burst out laughing. The sound bounced all over the room. An older guy in uniform looked in at the door for a few seconds, then went away without a word.

'Your wife is missing, Mr Quinn,' Clint said, 'and you're laughing. Can you explain that?' And he glanced over at the jockey, who just shook his head and reknotted his hands.

If Jackie had been there she could have told them that I always laugh when things are really bad. I laughed at my own sister's funeral – can't get much worse than that. Poor Lisa. 'You're a stupid sod, Robbie Quinn,' Jackie had whispered under her breath, passing me a folded handkerchief. And I'd sobbed and tittered into the green tartan and everyone except Jackie moved a little bit away, so that when my poor sister was safely out of sight I found myself almost alone, as if I'd been at someone else's graveside, a different funeral. The smell of the fresh-turned earth that day was oddly pleasant. When the vicar walked back and said, 'Can I help you, Mr Quinn?' I let Jackie answer for me. 'I'm taking him home now,' she said, and she slipped her hand under my arm and led me towards the road. Tender. Sometimes things could be really tender between us. We actually walked home that day, though it was miles. Halfway there, where the road bends away from the edge of town like it's trying to escape all the dullness, I threw the handkerchief into the Torrens. For once, Jackie didn't say a word, just did up her top button where a sharpish breeze was pushing in. When I turned back to the water, the handkerchief was floating away like a small, checked raft.

*

Four miles. That's the distance between here and the hospital. I know it's supposed to be kilometres but Jackie never broke the habit of talking in miles, so I kept it, too. I never walked to my shift, not once, but Jackie liked walking. We didn't use the car for work. 'I hate those smelly buses,' she'd say. 'And those rotten sods, ripping us off with the parking.'

I wouldn't let her walk at night, and she'd moan about that sometimes, insisting there were too many freaks on the bus. But she'd humour me.

'Take a taxi if you miss the last bus,' I'd tell her.

'Yeah, yeah, moneybags,' she'd answer.

There are only two street cameras between the hospital and our house. One points at the footpath, one at the road. You learn this stuff. On the night she disappeared, Jackie was picked up on both of them, walking quickly. On the second one, she stops and unbuttons her jacket because she's got too warm. She's hurrying because she's late leaving the hospital and it's pretty dark, except for the light from Roy's Discount Meats spilling into the road.

They showed me the camera footage of Jackie a couple of times. I could hear Clint breathing beside me as I watched, could feel his eyes on the side of my face. As Jackie walks out of view – the last sight of her – her coat, which is slung over one shoulder, lifts in the wind like a purple cape. She looks back, as if someone has called her. Then she turns towards home, stepping into a great pool of darkness.

★

Truth is, I was thinking about leaving her. There was never a big fight, no major issue. Most of the time, to use Jackie's words, we *mucked along* pretty well. I just wanted to find a bit of peace on my own. I like my own company, always have. At work, the night shifts used to kill some of the others, but not me. I liked the hush that came over the ward late at night. It's always had a magical quality, like anything was possible. But maybe, on the quiet nights, there was too much time to think. And sometimes, I admit it, I thought about a life without Jackie.

My feeble half-notions about leaving her make me cringe now. It all seems so petty, after everything that followed.

'I thought you were starting early today,' I said to Jackie as she sat down at the breakfast table on our last day together.

'Phoned in sick,' she said.

Her voice was tight. She hadn't brushed her hair, which was unusual. She was hugging her coffee cup with two hands, holding it so hard that I thought it might crack open and slosh over us both. I ate my toast and watched her, the crunching loud in my ears. Jackie knew about Ida Costello in Bed 6, I could see that. She was never off that damn phone of hers.

'I can't stay here now,' she said, staring. 'You know I can't get up every day and look at you, after what went on.'

I was surprised at how angry she was. 'Christ, Jackie, she was nearly ninety. The woman had one lung. She was in a lot of—'

'Don't say it!' Jackie actually shrieked those words. Later, our neighbour would tell Clint he heard it, clear as a bell. We weren't shouters, generally.

Jackie was up on her feet then. She walked over to the window and stood there for a long time, her back to me. Then she turned and said, very quietly, '*You* don't get to choose these things, Robbie Quinn ... And you decided about Lisa, didn't you?'

She could see by my face it was true.

'Your own sister, for God's sake.' Jackie seemed very small, standing there in her dressing gown, her balled fists like little apples in the pale pink pockets. 'And poor old Ida. She was a prisoner of war.'

I started to move towards Jackie but she looked like she might jump through the window if I came any closer.

'So, it was you all that time at Welgrove General, wasn't it?' she said. I was close enough to see her eyes fill with tears. 'That big woman with the sarcoma, and poor old Mrs Lacey. Christ, Robbie, you *killed* those people.'

'Jackie,' I said, but more words wouldn't come.

She was staring at me with repulsion. 'You covered it up well,' she said, her voice suddenly nurse-calm.

Evelyn Lacey's face loomed at me out of the past. Relieved. That's how she'd looked. There was a bit of talk after she died – that nosy new registrar – but nothing came of it and we both left Welgrove soon afterwards.

Now, looking at Jackie's disgusted face, I didn't know whether to feel angry or sad. I thought she'd realised about

Lisa. 'It's for the best,' Jackie said at the time, when my sister was finally gone. 'The best.' But now I could see the truth: Jackie's words weren't some coded message of approval. *For the best* was just another cliché. Hospitals are full of them. Doctors, nurses, counsellors. Even the tea lady never shuts up. It's what we say when we can't make things better.

Jackie had never mentioned the deaths at Welgrove until that day, after Ida Costello died. Not in any specific sense. Any blaming sense. But something must have clicked for her with Ida's death. Everything seemed obvious to her then.

'How could you?' she said, breaking down, fleeing towards the bedroom. I knew she'd leave. In the doorway, only half turning as if she could no longer bear to look at me, she said, 'It's murder, you stupid fucking sod.'

I wasn't sorry about Ida Costello. 'Say a prayer for me, won't you?' Ida used to say, most days. I told her I wasn't religious, every time, but she'd just say, 'Well, maybe today.' She wasn't hoping to get better – she knew enough to know that wouldn't happen. She was hoping she'd die. That's what all these hypocrites can't accept, what Jackie could never accept: these people had had enough. My poor cancer-raddled sister wanted to die. 'Help me, Robbie,' she said, and I knew exactly what she meant. But helping Lisa didn't come easily. It's much more straightforward when they're just patients.

Welgrove General is a big country hospital: wide wooden verandahs at the front, farmland in one direction, bush in the other, wallabies on the back lawn of an evening. Beautiful place. I met Jackie there, and we stayed six years before we moved to Adelaide. But Welgrove General is like every other hospital: people get sick, people get better, people die. Jackie was wrong about one thing, though. Yes, there was the woman with the rhabdomyosarcoma – Trudy was her name – and poor old Evelyn Lacey with everything under the sun. But Frank Easton was the first. He was a retired barley farmer, massive guy, never smoked a day in his life, sang in the local choir. Bone cancer – primary – then it raced through his body. Yet he was the man who would not die.

One night, late, Frank rang the call button. The pain must have been bad. He asked me, straight out, to finish him off. You'd be surprised how common that is. I gave him the usual blather: told him it was impossible, strict protocols, rules, laws. He grabbed my wrist, still a surprisingly strong grasp. He looked directly at me, as much as he could. The rain was striking the roof so hard I could barely hear him.

'Find a way,' he said.

So I did. Odd how I didn't give it much thought at the time. It felt like a job to be done, just like all the other jobs. Drugs, of course. What else? There's not a thing I don't know about them. The doctors think the nurses haven't got a clue but, honestly, it's usually the other way around. It's a point of pride for me: three generations of pharmacists and a couple of secret addicts thrown in for good measure. I knew what I was doing.

'All the best, Frank,' I said to him. I felt faintly nervous when it was over. But there was no trouble. Poor old Frank was out of his pain and no one suspected a thing. Not even Jackie.

But Frank had a son, a surly little bastard called Frank Junior who'd come up to the hospital most days, always making sure his father's finances were sorted in his favour. Day after day he'd sit by the bed, buttoning down every last corner of the farm and all the rest. In a weak moment, old Frank was fool enough to tell him that he was thinking of approaching one of the nurses on the late shift to finish him off. I think I actually walked in on them having this conversation.

'Don't be stupid, Dad,' Frank Junior told him, as I came towards them. 'You've got the solicitor coming in tomorrow. The house thing.' Old Frank hushed him with a waving hand, and Junior sat glowering at me from beside the bed, saying no more. Of course, I had no idea what this meant at the time.

But it turns out old Frank didn't want Junior – who must have been fifty, at least – to get the family home. He was going to inherit pretty well everything else, but the house was going to Frank's niece, not his son. She'd come in, late afternoon on that final day, and left in tears. Real tears. Frank had made his decision; after that he was ready to go.

The following morning, as I was packing up the room – old Frank's body had been moved downstairs – Junior came in behind me, closed the door.

'Think you're pretty clever, don't you?' he said, standing very close. I could smell his toothpaste. He was a severe asthmatic; I could hear the pull in his chest as he waited for my response. The barley farm was going to kill him, I thought, with some satisfaction. I didn't turn around, just kept packing up the kit.

'I know it was you,' he said. His father was barely cold and it was pretty obvious that he'd already had word that he didn't get the house in town. 'I'm going to make you sorry, Nurse Quinn,' he said.

Junior was smart enough to know that he could never prove anything, medically. He had taken a long, hard look at me from his perch in the corner of his father's room and rightly guessed I had everything covered. But I remember thinking, as his eyes followed me around the room each day, that he might be a man who could make real trouble. In a hospital, you get rather good at analysing people. You see everything across those beds. Frank Junior was a hater, I saw that; a vindictive little hater. And I let that slide. I only made one mistake, but it was a big one: I put Frank Junior out of my mind.

'Do you remember a guy called Easton. From Welgrove?' Jackie said one night, warming up a curry after her shift.

I felt my heart race. 'Easton? No.'

'Yes, you do,' she said. 'The barley farmer. Frank Easton. Malloy Ward. The one who used to sing sometimes. Hung on for ages, poor sod.'

'Oh, yeah. What about him?'

'Remember he had a son?' Jackie said. 'Wiry little guy, about fifty. Not very nice. Came in all the time.'

'Vaguely,' I lied.

'Saw him this evening.' Jackie was banging sticky rice off the spoon, making an incredible racket. I'd already eaten. I was sipping a beer, watching her from across the table. 'He was called Frank as well,' she said. 'Remember? Frank Junior.'

'Junior?' I said, keeping my voice flat.

'Yeah. He was on the bus,' she said, crashing her cutlery onto the table. Was there ever a moment, I wondered, when Jackie was doing something quietly?

I took another sip. 'It wouldn't have been him. Didn't he inherit the old man's farm? That's a day's drive away. What would he be doing in the middle of Adelaide?'

'Would have made a pretty puny farmer if you ask me,' she said, forking in the curry. 'Bet he sold it, or went bust. Anyway, it was definitely him. Don't you remember he had a tattoo on his hand? Um ...' She held up her hands to work out where she'd seen it on him. 'His left hand. A little thistle. A red and green thistle down near his thumb. You must have noticed it. It was definitely him.'

'Where did he get off?' I said, remembering the tattooed hand lying flat on his father's bed. I turned my beer bottle in its pool of condensation. Jackie had pulled the newspaper towards her and wasn't listening. 'Jackie!'

She jumped. 'Jesus, what's wrong with you? I don't

know. Oh, yes I do – the same stop as me. After me. He didn't see me, though. He was reading something on the bus. I only saw the tattoo when I was getting off.'

The beer suddenly seemed too cold, sending a shiver to my brain. 'Did he walk the same way as you?'

She looked up from the paper. 'Hmm? No. He didn't walk anywhere. He sat down at the bus stop and was looking for something in a bag. I saw him when I crossed the road.' Turning to me, serving spoon in hand, she said, 'Want some more curry?'

Jackie's been listed as missing for six years now. A cold case, they call it. Clint retired to a walnut farm. He's squinting at aphids these days, I guess. There was one journalist who used to arrive on my doorstep every year around the date of Jackie's disappearance. The last time I saw him I surprised myself by asking him in, making him coffee. He got chatty, told me he wrote about the economy, mostly, but he was keen to get into investigative work, write a book. He told me he was examining Jackie's case as a kind of hobby. A hobby. I knew I had to pack up when I heard that, leave Adelaide for good. I was starting to feel rage rather than pity, and rage didn't look like a logical reason to kill someone.

Melbourne's the kind of city to get lost in, only I know pretty well every street these days. I drive a taxi. Seriously. No more hospitals for me. Taxi driving's harder than it looks: long hours and some pretty despicable people, drunk and sober. Nice ones, too, of course, and some days, if I'm in the mood and they mention some affliction, I give them a free consultation. There's always a good tip at the end of those rides.

There's a coffee shop near the train station where I used to go regularly, mostly because none of the other drivers stop there. It was winter, I remember; everyone had coats on. I'd bent my head to take a careful sip of coffee – it's always served scalding hot there – and I heard a voice I knew behind me. 'Ham and cheese, not ham and tomato.' A man, pissed off, complaining about his toasted sandwich. The girl behind the counter apologised and gave him his money back when he wouldn't wait for a replacement. I didn't turn my head, just hunkered down inside my collar, kept the coffee mug close to my face. Had he seen me? All I saw was the back of a man in a longish navy coat and a red beanie. A woman with a twin pram carved up any further view of him as he left, but, standing up, I could see him at the corner. He didn't look back. I watched as he pulled one of his gloves off with his teeth to sort out his money. Even from that distance, I could see the dark blob of tattoo near his wrist as he walked towards the train and disappeared.

I knew there was a chance Frank Junior could be in Melbourne. I'd met old Frank's niece – the one who got the house – when I went back to the area for my mother's funeral. She came to the service. 'Thank you for being so good to Uncle Frank,' she said, pressing my hand in the overheated chapel.

'He was a far better man than I'll ever be,' I said. That was true. Later, she told me the barley farm was gone. 'Junior sold it for half nothing. Said he hated the country. Said farming was for idiots.'

I didn't see Frank Junior again for a long time. I drove. I had good days and bad days. I waited. I dreamed – literally dreamed – of him getting into my cab without realising it was me at the wheel. I had special locks fitted, just in case.

It took me almost a full day before I finally twigged about the man I'd seen in the lane. I was at home, drinking coffee, staring out the window. Scenes from the previous few days were looping through my mind – that nice big tip from old Ingrid, the Scottish guy with one arm, the truck rollover on Hodda Terrace – all the jumble and flare of ordinary life. And then, half watching someone in the street lugging a shopping bag, I realised what I'd seen the night before: the man with the rubbish bag, the way he walked, the way he turned. The thought stunned me. At last. That man was Frank Junior.

It was a Thursday night. Late-night shopping; busy for me, most times. I was thinking about Jackie, if you can believe that. I'd gone a fair while without giving her too much thought, then for a week or so she'd kept coming into my mind. *Robbie Quinn. Robbie Quinn.* Pecking away at me, just like before.

I found Frank Junior's flat above a noodle shop. I almost laughed out loud when I pulled the corner of an envelope out of his mailbox and I saw his new name: just one letter stuck on the front of his old name. Frank Neaston. Pathetic. At least I'd had the decency to change mine completely.

Frank Junior always took his rubbish out last thing at night. It's never a good idea to be predictable.

His death didn't get any more coverage than it deserved. *A body discovered … a laneway off Drummond Street … the schoolboys are receiving counselling … not believed to be suspicious.* So said the woman on the news. The next night she announced that the body had been identified as Frank Neaston, retired labourer. I chortled. Frank Junior never laboured for anything in his life, except maybe that last breath. I used ketamine, mostly. Not ideal, but my options are limited these days. Not much of the stash I took from Welgrove left now. I used a hypodermic, of course. It was late; I knew he'd be dead by the time he was found.

The TV showed a long shot of the laneway. The woman from the noodle shop was leaving a bunch of flowers. I was amazed to see she got the spot exactly right: just left of the big wheelie bin.

'He came in on Tuesday nights,' she said to the camera, standing awkwardly close. 'Beef noodles.'

The camera panned across a small crowd of bystanders staring down the now-empty lane. A couple of kids chewing gum, a tall man, a few women. The reporter, a young guy with a square thatch of red hair, signed off, 'Back to you, Elena.'

And then it was over. I'd been watching all this, mulling over the mixed feelings I was having: relief, pleasure, that odd flatness. I was half thinking that I might move back to Adelaide now that everything was settled. Now that there was no more danger of being exposed.

The faces of the crowd in the laneway faded into the next piece of news. Suddenly, I was on my feet. One of the women in that crowd. The one with the white jumper. It couldn't be. The way she turned her head, her chin in profile, her hands balled in her pockets. It was Jackie.

Every day I tell myself it was not her. A look-alike, that's all. *Jackie's dead and you know it.* I say that over and over. I work hard at keeping everything tamped down. I force her out of my mind. The look on her face. Her voice. I think of nothing, just sit at the window and watch the world go by.

After Frank Junior – after Jackie – I thought I'd feel … free. I thought the past could be filed away and forgotten. A bit of peace. That's all I've ever wanted. But when I empty my head, that's when I hear it. *Robbie Quinn. Robbie Quinn.* In a crowd, especially, I hear that voice. And when I spin around, my eyes raking through all the bodies, I'd swear I catch a glimpse of her face, turning away.

The News

When the news came to the house, it slipped in quietly, past the smiling and the bottles and the happy chink of glasses, deaf to the music pushing at the walls. For a moment, it watched a tall man holding a bottle by the neck, calling, 'No, not that! Play this one next,' but it moved on. It could smell perfume, wine, a warm trace of spice, bodies. There was laughter, which always made it uneasy. A woman said, 'It's totally true,' and a group guffawed and shook their heads. 'God!' one of them said. The news stepped by on tiptoe.

At first, no one noticed the small circle of hush at the end of the room; the way it stood, mesmerised and breathless. A woman with dark hair turned towards the news, buckling without warning, hands catching her as she fell, folding her into a chair, a thin arc of red wine on the carpet, vivid as a wound. And how disquiet can lap across a room, freezing everything in its path: the head tipping back to laugh, the fingers reaching for food, the reluctant child being taken outside.

All the faces turned to the woman, watching her being helped to her feet, led to the door, the news winding around her shoulders, tight and sinuous. And when they looked away, there was something obscene about those paper lanterns, the gaudy shine of the bows, the winking summer lights on the porch. Only the music played on, ringing out like a strange and terrible profanity until someone shouted, 'Turn it off, for Chrissake, shut it down.'

And then she was gone. The last of a pale dress in the doorway. Stillness. Only the sound of a child, wailing in the garden. 'I want to go home.'

Things

There are no neighbours. That's important. Old Mr Novak, who lived on the other side of our walls for decades, is long gone. I still miss hearing snatches of his beautiful baritone and, just once, a heartbreaking violin. When I mentioned this he shook his head and said, 'No, no, my dear, there was no violin. It must have been the radio,' and asked about my sister. I told him Lottie was fine, and changed the subject. But after all the years separated by a narrow seam of brick and ageing plaster, I knew his bedroom was the mirror image of my own. The sound of the violin was unmistakable. No matter. We all have our secrets.

I have only three houses to consider. Our house, the one on the end, once belonged to a typically English terrace of red-brick homes, all curving slightly to the left like a wheeling regiment of soldiers. Our parents had just moved in when German bombers reduced two of the houses and their occupants to smoking rubble. The gap remains, filled by a half-hearted children's play area. Mr Novak's place is still empty. While his nephews wrangle over their inheritance, the house waits quietly, unperturbed, its window blinds firmly down.

The third house in our truncated row is also empty, but not for long. It's just been sold. There's an article in the local newspaper, here in front of me. A neat young man in a buttoned-up shirt, smiling into the camera. *Chess prodigy makes a move on renovation.* There's new blood coming into the neighbourhood, a sense of all that is old and dull being swept away. Cleansed. This is entirely right.

Our house was big, once. Especially the front room, with its bay window and a great square rug, wide enough to lie across. One year, when Lottie and I were small, we had a Christmas tree in the far corner. The last of its trunk is in the back garden somewhere.

By the time Lottie was seventeen, there was still a little bit of space left in the front room. I remember her sitting in there, perched on the armrest of the old navy sofa, looking out the window. That year, the local school band was playing across the street, collecting money in a woven basket. A sign on the grass verge explained that they were saving for a coach trip to London. Carols. It didn't feel cold enough for Christmas carols. The snow came much later that winter. The snow that changed everything.

I can still picture Lottie watching passers-by gravitate towards the band. 'They're putting money in the basket, Jenny,' she told me. She was pleased, but she was getting overexcited. She said she could see the mean woman. That was the old hag from the sweet shop. Lottie had gone in there once, but she got her words into a muddle and the woman wouldn't serve her. 'I can't make out what you're saying, girly,' she said to Lottie. 'You're talking gibberish.' She told her to come back with a responsible adult.

'Look, Jenny, look!' Lottie called out that day. When I went to the window, I could see the sweet-shop woman hanging back, one misshapen arm holding on to a wrought-iron fence. She kept so many tissues balled in her cardigan sleeves that they looked like tumours under the wool.

'She's getting music for free!' Lottie was shouting and pointing. 'She's stealing it!'

I told Lottie there was no rule about having to give money, that it was voluntary, but she started jumping on the sofa, yelling 'Stealing, stealing' until I came and calmed her. She was wearing our grandmother's necklace. A heavy gold chain with a crescent-moon pendant, its inner curve edged with tiny red stones. As Lottie jumped and shouted, the chain flew up, its bright paring of moon suspended, for a moment, before she fell to earth again.

'Indian rubies,' our grandmother had told us in a whispery voice when we'd first seen that necklace. 'My wedding present from your dear grandfather.' Lottie and I had watched, transfixed, as the gaudy moon bobbed under her fingers.

After Grandma died, our mother said, 'Garnets, if they're real stones at all,' and dropped the necklace into an old box under the hall table. She had a way of pulling the air out of a room, of filling it to the brim with negative things.

After the band played on the corner, Lottie never went into the front room again. A young couple with bulky shopping bags had stopped at the gate to rearrange their parcels. They noticed Lottie waving and calling out. But the couple seemed to sense something wasn't right and the man put his arm around the woman and turned her away. Poor Lottie got very upset. It was too much for her. I made her stay in the back kitchen after that. She could be peaceful there.

The old sofa is still in the front room, though I haven't seen it for years. There's no view from the window anymore. Not long ago I squeezed in there, and I could hear children outside, bouncing a ball. There was something about those sounds: the slap, slap of the rubber on the pavement, a screechy girl, the way another one laughed – a big, throaty laugh – that reminded me of Lottie. I felt too sad to be standing there, so I worked my way back to the hall, pulling the door behind me as much as I could. I won't go in there again. It will be like Mr Novak's house, like our parents' room, like Lottie's room: places that have closed their eyes forever.

Lottie is dead. She was always so vibrant and dramatic that it's hard, even now, to accept how plain her death was. There was no rare and terrible disease, no violence, no deadly sting from a creature that had sailed halfway around the world in the nib of a banana. If I had known how awful a plain death could be, I would have wished for some glossy black spider to find its poisonous way in here. Make it quick.

★

When the snow finally came that year, it filled the back garden, softening the boxy edges of things into something less jagged and imposing. Snow piled up on the front path, clouded the windows, muffled the grind of the town. We were cocooned inside the house, and quite calm. There was always food. The pipes froze, but we had boxes of bottled water that had been stacked in the pantry when our parents were alive. Towards the end of that week, someone made their way to our front door and knocked for a long time. I think they may have pushed something through the letterbox. Later, from the corner of an upstairs window, we could see how the snow on the front path had been trampled and pushed aside. We both stared at the old wooden gate left open to the street.

Lottie loved winter. Even when she was a small child she never seemed to feel the cold. I can barely recall her wearing a coat or gloves. She hated the heat. When she was about eleven, there was a very hot summer. One long, stifling night she called out repeatedly from her bed, 'Too hot. No air,' and banged on the wall with the flat of her hand.

She was so happy when the big snow came. Gusts of wind drove it onto the windows, where it splattered against the glass like the limbs of a flying insect. Sometimes the snow fell straight down, silent and endless. Lottie was spellbound. There was a high, narrow window in the back kitchen with one of the big dining-room chairs underneath it. Lottie would teeter on the pile of newspapers stacked on the seat, watching the snow fall in the back garden.

'Charlotte! Get down and pull that window closed,' I'd tell her. 'There's a terrible draught.'

But Lottie would push her face through the small opening and gulp in the freezing air, trying to catch flakes of snow on her tongue. She'd stand on that chair for hours at a time. It was becoming harder to keep her calm. It sometimes suited me to leave her there, her face glowing and ruddy with cold.

It began with the heating-oil men. Two of them: one not much older than Lottie, the other middle-aged. 'Did you see the state of the place?' I heard the young one say. 'Christ, how does anyone live like that?'

The older man was pulling the oil hose back towards the truck. 'Nutters,' he said. 'And my old girl thinks I'm bad. Can't wait to tell her about this lot.'

I was standing at the dining-room window, listening to every word they said. They couldn't see me with all the boxes stacked against the glass. The boxes were empty; I'd been keeping them for the local kindergarten. I could hear the men outside, breathing in the cold air, the hose dragging on the ground.

'You'll need to get a signature,' I heard the older man say. 'Go to the back door,' he said. 'The older one is half normal. Here, take my pen. You'll be drawing the fucking pension before they can find one in that mess.'

The younger man, whose front teeth were bucked, was still chuckling when he appeared at the door. I signed without saying a word. Lottie was calling out, 'Thank you, thank you, oil man,' from the hallway.

'You'll be nice and snug now,' he said to me, kindly enough, before closing the folder. But I heard them laughing as they went back down the path. The sound of the truck roaring away left a mark on my heart.

The buck-toothed boy was right: we were nice and snug that winter. Just me and Lottie, curled like hedgehogs in our chairs. We had everything we needed in that back kitchen. We boiled the eggs that Mr Novak left for us in a padded bag by the side gate. We had our beans, and I found some lime cordial that Lottie would have drunk neat if I hadn't stopped her. I'd given up buying the newspaper by then, but I had a tiny radio that I listened to when the gales were blowing. *Rockall. Hebrides. Becoming cyclonic. Bailey. Fair Isle. Cyclonic at times.* The thought of those turbulent places, the unstoppable, chaotic forces sweeping across them, was oddly soothing. It was the hardest winter for seventy years, the radio told me: motorways were closed, there were pile-ups, people stranded in freezing cars. Watching Lottie beside me, sleeping peacefully in her chair, made me feel lucky, for a while.

Sometimes, dreadful mistakes only become clear when everything is lost. This old house has two floors, three if you count the attic, although I haven't been able to get up there for years. When it got so cold that even Lottie was starting to feel the chill, I turned the heating up to maximum without a thought. Much later, I realised every radiator in the house was going at full tilt, warming rooms we'd not been in for years. We stripped off our layers while the snow continued to tap against the windows. It felt like we had warmth enough for the entire terrace, the town, the whole world. Even the attic must have had some sort of heating because I've never seen so many birds in our back garden, swooping down onto the icy branches of trees, then back up to the warm slate of our roof. Dozens of them. Hundreds.

It's surprising how quickly a house goes cold. And the quiet that comes when the throb of the machinery ceases. The birds left first. A large flock curved above Mr Novak's house, then disappeared. Lottie didn't complain, even though she pulled out an old school cardigan of mine and wrapped it around her neck like a scarf. I told her there was no oil left. 'Get the man,' she said. The young fellow had grinned at her with his great, square teeth and she had not forgotten. But I kept hearing their laughter on the side path, kept seeing their faces at the back door. How their eyes had widened in surprise. The shocked glance they'd exchanged before turning to their work.

The empty house beside Mr Novak's place was once a teacher's house. He was no relation to us although we shared the same family name.

'Looks like this is going to be the Greene end of the terrace,' the postman, who was universally known as Call-Me-Johnny, sang out as I passed one day. He'd been ringing the front doorbell of Number 29 but getting no answer.

'Another Greene just moved in here, by the looks of it,' he said to me. 'Unless of course you've got a' – he read the label – 'Simon Greene tucked up in your place, Jennifer?'

'I'm afraid that's me.' A middle-aged man in a pale blue shirt appeared at the door, looking slightly flustered. 'Sorry, I was in the back garden,' he said.

'There's Greene everywhere!' Call-Me-Johnny said, quite delighted with his silly quips. He pointed to me. 'This lady's Greene, too. Lives two doors up.'

I was eager to get away but the man took the parcel and stepped down to the front gate to introduce himself.

'Delighted to meet you,' he said, as we exchanged names and shook hands. He had a pair of reading glasses tucked into his shirt pocket. He nodded at the parcel he'd pinned under one arm. 'Another book,' he said, ruefully. 'Don't seem to be able to resist.' He had dark brown hair, quite short, except for a long sweep of fringe with a few strands of silvery grey. 'I'll have to cut back on my addiction now that I've bought this place.' He had a nice voice.

'Oh blimey, not another book lover!' Call-Me-Johnny was still standing beside us. 'You'll be the death of me, you lot,' he said, staggering on the footpath in mock horror, before chuckling to himself and walking away, patting his heavy satchel like the head of a large dog.

We laughed then, the two of us, new neighbours and soon-to-be friends. Just a few years after that, books would be ordered online and exhausted couriers in lurid trucks would ply this road. Call-Me-Johnny, finding nothing funny in his new work contract, would take voluntary redundancy and retire to Blackpool. But the first time I met Simon is set fast in my mind. The two of us smiling, watching the postman make his way down the terrace, Simon's hand on the gatepost, the wrapped book under his arm. And the way we said, 'Yes, an amazing coincidence … common enough name, for sure, but still.' And how we talked about books, free-falling into that vast canopy of stories. 'Oh yes, I've read it,' and, 'I was a little disappointed with her last novel but I couldn't put her new one down,' and, 'Absolutely, an incredible story; I was crying by the end of it. It was brilliant. Just brilliant.'

If I could choose my final thought on this earth, it would be that scene, for the innocent happiness it brought me. The two of us, together, smiling. When I think of it, I am a shining, iridescent creature, caught with him forever in smooth amber. Extinguished, yet perfect.

Someone was at the front door, knocking. I wasn't afraid. It was not unusual for charity collectors or other strangers to let themselves into the front garden. I ignored it, as I always do. That door hasn't been opened for years.

Strange how people who want something always knock the same way: three assertive knocks, silence, two more knocks, silence. After a long pause, I'd hear the gate creak, then nothing. When I think back on it, the knocks I heard that day were different: more tentative, uncertain. But then the silence came, and I relaxed again.

A few minutes later, I heard footsteps. Someone was walking down the path at the side of the house. Even then, I was unconcerned. I was in my chair in the back kitchen. I won't make a sound, I thought. No one can see me from here.

Then I remembered the robin. It was an unseasonably warm day. Early autumn. A large robin had perched on the old washing machine outside. I had watched it for a long time. It didn't move, just tilted its plain, bronze head to and fro, its red chest flaring in the light.

I had left the back door open. The footsteps rounded the corner of the house.

'Jennifer? Hello. Jennifer? Are you there?'

The voice was unmistakable. It was Simon. I felt panic shoot through my body. If he moved any closer to the door, he would see me.

He was wearing the same blue shirt he'd had on when we first met. He smiled when he spotted me. I treasure that. He had a parcel in his hand, clearly a book.

'Jennifer!' he said in a pleased, slightly relieved voice. And then he said, 'Oh!' loud and fast, stepping back from the doorway as if the threshold were an unexpected cliff. His free hand slapped against his throat but it was too late to trap the sound of his shock.

For one precious moment, he had seen only me. Then he saw everything else. And it was just like the oil men, the way his eyes took in all the things. Without moving, without so much as turning my head, I saw what he saw. He was breathing like a man who had run a long way.

'I'm so sorry,' he said, quietly. He held up the parcel. 'The postman. Got it wrong. Wrong Greene, I mean.' He took another step backwards. 'It's a book. I … I didn't mean to intrude.'

I stood up. We faced each other on either side of the doorway. Simon was forcing his gaze away from the room and back to my face.

'I thought I'd leave this by the back door but then … I saw … it was open,' he said, his face blazing.

I felt a surge of absolute fury. I wanted to step across that threshold and pummel him, rip that book apart and grind it under my shoe. He had wrecked everything by coming here. I'd played a careful game. Small deceptions that meant we met in the street, in a cafe or at the library. I'd had coffee in his house. I told him an ancient aunt of mine lived here, that visitors disturbed her. And it had been wonderful. All those stories, those books. We'd built great walls of book talk around us. There was no romance. I wondered a few times whether he might be gay. I didn't care. I was glad to have a friend.

I heard myself say, 'I don't think you should come here again, Simon.'

He pressed his lips together. 'No,' he said. He cast about briefly for some flat surface to put down the book. There was none. Seeing that, he held it out to me. I took the terrible weight of it in my hand. 'I'm so very sorry,' he said, before walking away.

I was still standing in the doorway when he reappeared.

He stopped a few steps from the back door. I could see the robin on a pile of wood near him. It seemed as if years had passed.

'Jennifer,' he said. 'I could help you.'

It was then I felt it. The terror. I felt those walls of rubbish behind me, above me. All at once they seemed to move, flex, like powerful muscles. Like a house come to life with things. In the maze of boxes, it knew where I was, squeezed into this corner of the kitchen, the door in front of me my last escape. All I had to do was step forward, reach out, cross that threshold. Simon would take my hand. He was a good man. He would help me. But the house, this house I had reshaped into something terrible, was contracting against me. Even the floor seemed to wrap around my feet like a sinuous vine.

Simon moved closer. 'I'm worried about you,' he said. 'Being here. And your aunt. It's not safe.'

Despite his best efforts, I saw his eyes flit around the room.

'Jennifer, how would you both get out,' he said. 'What if something happened? If there was … a fire?'

A fire. And I felt my pulse race. A beautiful, cleansing fire to vanquish this monstrous place. It's astonishing how many boxes of matches are in this house.

'There is no aunt,' I said, amazed to hear my own robot voice.

Simon stared, took a deep breath. 'I see,' he whispered.

'I don't need any help, thank you, Simon,' I told him.

I felt a throb of life in the floor beneath me.

He was going to say more, I could see that, but after a moment he lowered his gaze. 'Very well,' he said. 'Jennifer, I'm so sorry I came here. I meant no harm.'

It was a strange, courtly end. I would not have been surprised if he'd bowed.

There is no going back. No returning to the Christmas tree, or the navy sofa on the big square rug. No Lottie spinning and jumping, catching snow on her tongue. 'So hot,' she'd said to me, in those last hours we spent together, the fever boiling within her. I didn't realise how sick she was until I heard the high, thin wheeze of her chest, filled to the brim.

When the ambulance men came, they noticed only Lottie. They did not care about things. They didn't look at me. Together, we stared at Lottie, lying limp in her chair. They lifted her up and carried her to the gurney at the door. Pneumonia, they said. Only Lottie looked back, her eyes half closed, willing me to make it better. So hot. No air. The wail of the siren in the street. And then she was gone.

There's no one left, now. I have built a new house here, with seams of paper and cloth, with walls as thick and heavy as a citadel. There've been times when these packed corridors, these rooms of things, have given me a kind of comfort, like the books around my bed when I was young.

'You'll disappear under those books, my girl,' my mother once said as I lay on the bed, reading.

'She's lost in all those silly stories,' I heard her tell my father.

After Lottie died, I became afraid of everything. The books could no longer console me. They loomed at me with their closed mouths, their pressed lips. I put boxes around them, covered them with newspapers. I did not think of Simon. In the local paper, there was a small photo of his house. *For sale. A beautifully kept garden*, it said. *Tranquil.* I thought about that word for a long time.

I'm curled here now, beside the boxes, the tins and jars, the magazines, all our old schoolwork. I have everything I need. I tuck Lottie's clothes around me, each garment scented with a ghostly trace of her.

The house feels glad again, released. It hums with the joy of things ending.

Speak the Words

I remember you in lipstick colours. Those cheap, brittle tubes heaped in a basket at the back of the chemist, down where they take in the prescriptions. The way your tired eyes might have fallen on them, your fingers scrabbling through the neon bursts of colour. Shocking pink, fiery tangerine, a heartbreaking red. I make the shape of you in the little mirror on the counter.

Once, at the bus stop, you turned to me as if about to say something, pressed your mouth into a thin line, and looked away. I heard the chink of bottles in your bag. Sometimes, I saw you at the library, backed into a corner, the flat of your head bobbing behind one of the old computers. And that last time, when we passed in the high street, before your house burned, before the smoke unfurled and waved like a flag above the edge of town.

I will take this one. The red. I will remember the pale circle of your face, the vivid slash of colour. The way your lips seemed to hover just ahead of you, as if they might shout down the road, speak the words you could not say.

The Mohair Coat

It could not go to strangers, this leaving coat. How could they know about the terrible newness of things? The way her parents had gripped the sleeves, a great rush of parting shaking them all. How they'd turned from her, then, without another word, bowing into the wind and the slick, grey road. And when the ship pulled away at last, streamers crosshatching the dock, how she'd watched them mount the old wharf steps, knowing by the set of their shoulders that they would not look back. As the ship rose beneath her feet, how she'd turned up her collar, watched the ocean unfold like a plan.

It could not be left for strangers, this returning coat. My mother's winter uniform for journeys back to her homeland. How she waved down to us, her hip pressed against the ship's rail, the sun burning her head, the coat looped over her arm like success. The seas waited and, later, the skies. Above the clouds, she tucked in the sleeves, made a pillow, watched the horizon for unforgotten places. She brought stories in her pockets.

It could not be handed to strangers, this quarantined coat, hovering like a ghost in a reek of naphthalene. Once, before the end, my mother took it out, laid it down on the bed like sorrow. The heat prickled the wool. I tried to imagine a place where the weight of this would feel right.

'Do you remember your mohair coat, Mum?' I said, and she ran her fingers across the lapel. I watched her shoulders rise and fall. She did not answer.

It could not stay with me, this haunting coat. I have travelled back to her country, carrying it in my arms. Better in a place where hard winds undo the mystery of double cuffs.

In the village, her ancient sister waits. *I look forward to meeting you*, she'd written in crafted loops. I will give her the coat. It has been worn four times in sixty years. We will not dare to speak of the unbearable brightness of its wool.

But in a post office two hours south, I can no longer bear the weight of empty clothes. I take the coat, cross the arms, lay it out on heavy card. In the overheated room, I watch the clock. Soon, a van cortège will come and carry it home along the roads of her youth.

As I seal the box, an impish scent of her – a stowaway in the hand-sewn lining – threads past me and is gone.

In that stifling room, wary eyes watch a stranger clasping a heavy coat, sobbing into its depths like an abandoned child.

Legacy

When it came at last, it was one hard push in the centre of his back. For an instant, he doubled over in a deep, elaborate bow. Fitting, somehow. There was no sound, save a single, thin exhalation, which may have belonged to one of us. His navy trench coat swaddled him as he drove down. A long pennant of maroon scarf, flying like the banner of a minor royal, waved in the air behind him. No arms flailed. Nothing unseemly. The water received him with a muted splash, pulled him down and away with the sea's sure hand. There was a moment, only one, when we told ourselves it was like a burial.

Nostrils. That's the first thing I recall. Mr Gregory had a plain English face: grey-blue eyes, fair skin, mousey brown hair worn surprisingly long. But his nostrils marked him. Great cavernous openings, permanently flared. You could see so far inside his nose it felt alarming. The interior was tinted in a wash of pale scarlet; a rare kind of hue, like the orchids Mum grew years ago, when she was happy.

Mr Gregory lived on our street. I often saw him ducking under his cottage doorway, or walking on the hill behind – striding, really, for he had a long-legged step that in a less serious man would have looked comical.

The best of our town lies behind his cottage. The land sweeps upwards in a velvet swathe, circling high above the buildings like a vivid green ruff. Braxman's Ridge at the top. It's all farms up there: sheep, horses, a few head of cattle. Good land. Wealthy people, if they'd ever sell, which they don't. Occasionally, when I was doing deliveries, I'd spot Mr Gregory from one of the back paddocks, stalking along the cliff path cut deep by a thousand years of walkers. The Atlantic breezes, close to pleasant in summer, would make his hair stand upright before patting it down with a slap.

From the top of the ridge, you can look back at the whole town, curled out of the wind like a sleeping cat. Ahead, there's a vast expanse of sea.

There's a seat at the highest point, an old metal bench. Long ago one of the legs worked itself free from its rusty shackle. It arches backwards, as if trying to step away from the hypnotising drop. Mr Gregory would sit there.

If other locals arrived, they'd recognise his dark coat and the beige curve of his hair, but they would not join him on the bench. Beside the man who never looked down, there seemed no space at all.

★

66

It was a Tuesday. I was in the new van. Justin usually did the afternoon farm run in the noisy blue bomb, but he'd backed into Grumpy Hedley's gate while gawping at his daughter, and we had to use the new one. Or I did. Justin still had whiplash, the fool.

The new van normally sat outside the shop, looking spruce in dark green and white. *Webster's Saddlery and Produce.* A large horse's head was painted on one side, an unnatural look in its flattened eye.

I didn't expect to see Mr Gregory. He didn't drive and, except for the cliff path, I never saw him out of town. He was heading downhill. I knew it was him, even from the back. It was the walk. Not exactly a goosestep but pronounced, jerky. Boys at school used to copy it, tucked in behind him on his way to class, the others sniggering.

Just as I passed him, I heard a single, loud shout. When I looked back, there was nothing. I turned in Grumpy's lower field and drove back up the road. Mr Gregory was lying motionless, pressed hard into a leafy hedge like an insect pinned to a board. He didn't seem conscious. I wasn't sure if he was alive.

'I'm fine,' he called, after a long silence.

I pulled up the van and ran across to him, words already clumping in my throat. I got my name out in something close to a shout. The rest was lost in stony mouthfuls of my usual hesitation.

'Oh, Peter, it's you,' Mr Gregory said, quite jovially, as if he'd just met me in Jury's Cafe.

He'd opened his eyes but hadn't moved. His nostrils, flaring pink, seemed to float above the bland ivory of his face.

'I'm alright, really. Just a slip,' he said.

I didn't trust myself with any more speech, so I looked for a dry foothold to help pull him up. Mr Gregory regarded me with a teacher's appraising look.

'Fenton, isn't it? Peter Fenton. I taught your brother. How is he?'

While he tested his limbs in small, balletic movements, I told him about Justin. How we'd both been at the saddlery since leaving St Bart's. Me first, Justin two years later. How we liked the work, dealing with the animals.

'Very good,' Mr Gregory said. He didn't seem to notice my stop-start sentences. He insisted he was completely unharmed, although his chin was badly scratched. I let him dust himself off. It didn't seem right to touch him.

'Can I drop you home, sir?'

Mr Gregory looked doubtfully at the van with its smirking horse's head, but he climbed in and we shot down Braxman's Hill and onto our road.

'You know I'm at the other end,' he said, into the embarrassed space that lay between us as we passed my house. We both glanced at the sagging roof, despite ourselves.

'I hope your mother is better now, Peter,' he said, without turning his head.

I could feel my words gathering in ragged formation. I nodded while I calmed myself; the old ruse. We thumped against the new speed bumps.

'Excellent,' Mr Gregory said, as if I'd just given him a full account of my family history. 'Well, it's been quite a day, Fenton,' he said.

A concrete path led to his front door, its edges lined with small, round stones, sunk halfway like rivets on a battleship. Mr Gregory unfolded his long legs and stepped out of the van. After shutting the door, he turned and squinted through the window.

'Will you come for a light tea, Peter? So I can thank you properly. Bring your brother. It would be nice to see Justin again. Thursday? Six? Excellent.'

He was gone. There'd been no time to answer. Justin had until Thursday to be out of that damn neck brace.

A light tea. I told Peter I wasn't going. No way. But my brother has a certain look that he gives me, without saying a word – and suddenly there I am, doing what he wants. We went along on the Thursday evening, me walking in behind him, glowering, my neck still throbbing. We both felt a bit awkward because Mr Gregory was still a teacher to us. History. Special subject: the War in the Pacific. We called him Greggers at school. He wasn't too strict, not mean like some of the psychos. He was a bit of a clean freak. He kept a bright blue cloth in his briefcase to wipe down his desk. He'd swoop it across the wood like an exotic bird before folding it carefully and pushing it into one of his bag's leather pockets. He kept to himself but everyone respected him. There was something untouchable about Mr Gregory.

He never taught Peter, who left St Bart's just after Dad was killed. It was supposed to be his last year of school. Things hadn't been going well for him, and his speech problems were getting worse. When Dad ploughed his new Harley into the railway bridge, Peter just fell apart. We all did, but Peter was the worst.

Old Charlie Webster took us under his wing. He'd known Mum for years – some connection with horses, way back. He offered Peter a job at the saddlery. Grandma kept saying it was a shame to see him leaving school early to go and work in a shop. Mum eventually snapped, shrieking that if Grandma hadn't pandered to her son's every whim, he wouldn't have been off making a fool of himself on a motorbike, leaving his family flat broke. Grandma took to quilting after that. Kept to her room.

Peter loved the saddlery. Dealing with horses calmed him. His stammering almost disappeared, except when that insufferable polo bunch came in, or when Grumpy's daughter, Lucy, came to see him. I used to fancy her myself. That's how I nearly broke my neck up at their farm, gawping at her while I was reversing. Two weeks in a neck brace was a high price to pay. She wasn't interested in me.

Hard to believe it, but we enjoyed that first trip to Mr Gregory's house. Mum had worried that he might be a bit strange, but it was fine. He was kind, and interesting to talk to. We told him about Dad, and all that came after that.

And it wasn't all doom and gloom. Sometimes, he could be quite funny. Well, witty. Clever. You wouldn't see it coming.

We always sat in the long sitting room. Mr Gregory usually had a fire burning, often well into summer. He liked the heat. There were three walls of ancient books in dark covers with a small, framed photo here and there. One picture looked like Mr Gregory as a young child, grasshopper legs in white lawn shorts, squinting into a bright sea.

There was always tea, properly brewed. Thin china cups with deep saucers. He taught us chess but we were both hopeless, sullying his beautiful wooden set with our clumsy moves. Mostly, we just talked, leaning into the hard-backed chairs, the brown leather creaking.

The room was painted an odd colour: a kind of dark orange. Above the fireplace, three model cars were parked in a neat line on the mantelpiece. Boyhood toys, I thought, given pride of place in a lonely man's front room.

He told us about his time in the Pacific. At school, he'd stuck to the facts pretty dryly, but when he finally talked about the horrific years he spent in a prisoner-of-war camp, we thought it was a shame that he couldn't speak of it as a teacher. There was a lot that he could not say.

We'd been calling on and off for over a year before he told us – eyes fixed on the model cars – what happened to his father. But the thing he kept from us the longest was what was happening to him.

'Liver, Fenton. Worst one of the lot. Typical. A legacy of the camp, they tell me. Going to get painful. Nothing to be done, of course. Too late for any treatment.'

That's how he told me. Just me. He wanted to protect Peter as long as possible from his own soft heart, from his tangle of words.

'Check the back gate for me, Peter, would you?' Mr Gregory had said. He had a morbid fear of vandals. We watched from the kitchen window as my brother made his way across the damp grass.

'I'm dying, Justin,' Mr Gregory said, without turning his head. 'I need your help.'

At the end of the garden, Peter gave us a thumbs-up sign. Mr Gregory raised his teacup to him. As I watched Peter walk towards us, I knew I was trapped. I wanted to run from that cottage, from the town, from everything that kept me here, protecting other people.

But I had to deal with it, the younger brother. Shield Peter, as I've always done. He'd got overly fond of Mr Gregory, and he wasn't going to take another loss well. I'd borne the full weight of Dad's death. Not Mum, not Peter. I identified Dad's body. I was just eighteen. Old enough, it turns out, to see your father lying dead with half his face staved in, the roots of his teeth showing on one side.

I was just a boy. It was too much to ask.

I think there's a time, in all bad things, when you wonder how it came to this. How a person who wanted a plain life, a plain-spoken life, could be here, at this terrible moment.

It was raining.

There was wind, of course, but the rain was a surprise; it had been dry for weeks. That was part of the plan: dry earth, no slips, no footprints. There was more light than we imagined.

We walked up in single file, keeping close to the seam of trees. Justin went first, then me. Mr Gregory followed behind, head bowed, legs working hard. We didn't speak.

Speed. That's what we needed. 'No silly nonsense,' he'd insisted at our final meeting. 'It's in everyone's interest for it to be quick.'

We stopped just before the metal bench and let Mr Gregory pass, as planned. He sat for a long time, staring ahead. We watched his back. A hank of his hair, caught by the wind, flapped to the wrong side of his head. I wanted to step forward and tidy the ungainly strands. Make it right for him.

But we did not move. There was a thin shrieking in my ears that I first thought was the wind, but this is how horror sounds. The worst part of it is the waiting.

Mr Gregory stood up. That was the sign.

The rain had slowed to the lightest mist. He made his way to the edge with unbearable slowness. It was not fear, I felt quite sure, but pain.

Close to the chosen point, his feet skidded, halting abruptly on a craggy tuft of wind-hardened grass.

I did not look at Justin. I could hear him breathing hard, above the wind, above the shrieking in my head.

Mr Gregory had thought of everything. We were to check no one was watching, then walk down just to the right of where he stood, where the last remnants of an ancient stone wall still clutched at the rocky edge. He would not look at us, even though we were approaching almost from the side. His right hand was up, palm facing out to sea.

I thought of the painting in the refectory at school: *The Light of the World*. William Holman Hunt. The fish pie on Fridays. The smell of boiled potatoes in the corridors. We ate under that picture. Had to write an essay about it. Did you know that the model for Jesus was a girl?

The rain stopped. The sea was crashing onto the rocks below. Mr Gregory lowered his hand. We did not move.

Justin pushed past me, rough and grunting. The earth came up. Tiny stones pressed into my face, cutting it with cruel, pointed teeth.

We painted out Charlie Webster's name and the smirking horse on the new van. A pair of backpackers bought the old blue bomb. We watched it groan up Braxman's Hill and out of our lives.

Funny how we still call it the new van; like us, it's getting on now. We'll need to repaint it again soon, retrace the fine lettering: *Fenton's Produce and Saddlery*. Peter will do it. He has a steady hand, these days.

Old Charlie sold the place to us when he retired. He still comes in to chat to the customers and berate us for what he calls our spendthrift ways. He and Mum still see each other, but she sticks to her old house and keeps him at a friendly distance. We did up the place for her, fixed the kitchen and the roof. She's happy there.

I'm just up the road if she needs me. The little cottage with the stones studded along its front path. It looks the same today, except we built on a room at the back when the babies were born. Mr Gregory's chair is still in the orange sitting room. Dark apricot, I'm told it's called. We had the chair re-upholstered. I never sit in it.

It was always going to be me. I see that now.

Who would have thought practicality could be such a deadly characteristic? Mr Gregory was a practical man. He found out he was dying when he was still at St Bart's, in my last year of school. The holidays he claimed he spent with his sister in Glasgow turned out to be multiple surgeries. Treatment, after all. But the cancer was unstoppable. Years as a POW taught him to gauge just how much his body could take. He timed it to perfection. But he could not act alone.

The Gregory family did not have a good war. Mr Gregory's father narrowly escaped the beheadings that came to most of his platoon. After the surrender of the Japanese, the family was reunited. They began again, apparently intact. But they were each disintegrating in their own reserved way, his father most of all.

'We thought they'd attack by sea,' Mr Gregory told me. 'That was the disaster.' No one dreamed that the Japanese would slash their way to Singapore through supposedly impenetrable jungle.

Years later, safe in their English house, his father hanged himself above his workbench. Mr Gregory, then a teenager, found him dangling above the toy cars he'd worked on to calm his mind. His mother buckled at the horror that came to her, at last, in an unremarkable red-brick street. She became obsessed with suicide, convinced that her son was planning it, the neighbours, the teachers, the Welsh woman at the library.

One hard winter she was found in her nightdress, beating on the door of the post office, convinced someone inside needed saving. On her deathbed, in a delirium of cancer and morphine, she begged her son never to do it.

And he could not. Fearless as he was, he would not go to the edge and jump. Nor could he bear the last horrors of an illness that had taken his mother before him. He needed someone practical. Someone like him, only young and strong. Someone already damaged enough to push a man off a cliff in cold blood. Someone who wouldn't flinch when his brother, finally knowing the plan, scattered the chess pieces across the table and sobbed like a lost child. Someone like me.

Mr Gregory did not fall on Braxman's Hill that first day. He had been waiting for me. Waiting for the sound of the old van, and the broken boy within it. He almost missed it, not listening for a new van, not bargaining on the fact that his saviour and killer was at home watching television in a neck brace.

Like us all, he did not bargain on complication. He did not expect to find a tongue-tied boy, an innocent, who could never, no matter what, push a man in the back and topple him over a cliff.

But a practical man thinks on his feet, and Mr Gregory saw, quickly enough, that the route to me was through Peter. It was a long game. I did not see it coming.

The return was good, you might say. Mr Gregory left a surprisingly large amount of money, for a teacher. He made sure the cottage went to me. He knew it would be me, in the end, up there on the cliff. The house is a comfortable place, and my wife, who thinks a practical man is a wondrous thing, loves its cosy rooms, its solid, dependable walls.

There were no suspicious circumstances. He'd left everything in order: a letter on the mantelpiece, tucked behind the cars, a copy posted to his solicitor. *To Peter and Justin Fenton, for their kindness in my final, difficult years.*

His older sister, whose existence we'd privately questioned, arrived on the overnight train that very day, as invited. We came for lunch, as instructed, to find an old woman with the same flared nose, holiday baggage slumped on the cottage path. Together we stirred our tea in his good cups as the search helicopter was buffeted along the sea's edge high above us.

She read at the funeral, her voice confident in her dead brother's draughty school chapel. She spoke of the family's suffering, how the English boarding school she'd dreaded had saved her from a similar fate. It was a dignified ceremony. Father Morrison talked a lot about mercy.

And life goes on.

Peter is a good businessman. Together we've built the saddlery into a thriving concern. The local newspaper covered his wedding last year.

I walk a bit now, to keep fit, to clear my head. The same deep path takes me up to the ridge; the same wind tugs at my sleeves. The bench has never been repaired: one gangling leg still threatens escape.

Sometimes, not often, I sit there.

On certain days, the days when I feel anger rising, that broken seat feels crowded, as if all the drowned ghosts have joined me to mourn what can't be undone. What can't be saved. They flit in the clean space before me, riding the thermals like glinting sea birds. They're beautiful. Mesmerising.

I wish they would carry away the touch of dark gaberdine. How smooth it was. Of a thin, hard spine beneath, yielding.

The water thunders far below. I never look down.

Thirty Years

They marry on a day of bountiful omens. A poltergeist wind harries the car, crashes the door shut on his hand. She wears a dress bequeathed by his mother. In an overheated room, they dance. The bridesmaids, slick in lilac upholstery, pull in their stomachs and hope for better. Her aunt, narrow-eyed, weighs him like a ham, does not smile as they pass.

The first year in, after a sly crack about the farm, he locks her outside. She pleads at the window as night falls. She avenges herself, exploring the culinary range of baked beans. Finds it broad.

A truce arrives: a year's worth of colic, the twins keening up the hall.

There's a question of a woman. A strange car seen outside the house, a neighbour squinting across the fields.

'It's not what you think,' he says, but will explain no further.

They do not speak of it, even now.

They leave their home of twenty years, down-sized

teenagers cursing under their breath. She leaned her head against the fireplace for the last time, wondered how they would fit into shrunken lives. While they waited in the car, he put his fist through the plaster, vowed never to drink another drop.

Today, an anniversary gift from the boys – young men now, dazed and half-happy in pensionable jobs. They hand over the plane tickets in a red envelope.

'Thirty good years,' they say.

When she sees the garish bow, stuck onto the corner with a great loop of tape, two fat tears slide down.

He says, 'Well, boys. How about that,' and pulls his milking jacket on.

She wonders whether he'll come; she might have to take her sister. But he digs out his suit and stretches it on the bed, where it lies like a flattened man.

Awkward in Paris, they will quarrel over steak served unexpectedly raw. Roses – *With the Manager's compliments* – will arc from the French windows, crosshatch the laneway like spent arrows.

On the journey home, storms will buffet the plane. She – reared in ancient, gripping soils – will be too afraid to speak. He, oblivious to disasters that have not arrived, will study his newspaper until the wheels touch down.

'Pleasant enough trip,' he'll say, when the engines cut. 'C'mon. Let's get going.'

He will not take her bag.

'Thank God I'm home,' he'll say, as she turns the key,

pushing hard at the door, which still sticks in one corner. 'I haven't had a decent feed for days.'

She'll shake her head and smile. 'You're quite impossible,' she'll tell him.

'True enough,' he'll say.

They'll go in. Make tea.

Cutting the Cord

Jackson Carter buys champagne on the way home from work. His first child – the secret one – has come of age.

He stands in the kitchen with his wife, staring past her into the garden. He winces at the thought of what those eighteen years have cost him. Since that pointless conference, all the ridiculous plush of the hotel, the sales guys jumping naked into the pool. No one where they ought to be.

The bottle feels heavy in his hand. Through the long window he sees it's a beautiful evening. Crisp, bright. He recalls himself up in the far corner of the garden, reading the letter. The way he'd stood, out of sight, looking back at the kitchen, the place lit up like a stage. He remembers the sprawl of the woman's handwriting. Marvels, for a moment, at that world without email, without phones small enough for hidden things.

Leaning against the garden shed, he'd pinched the edge of the paper as if it were on fire. *Pregnant. Baby.* In the thresh of words, that was all he saw. Then he'd vomited without warning by the compost heap. Pumpkins grow there now, their hooking tendrils advancing towards the house. They grow so fast.

The light is fading but he can still make out the serrations of the back wall, its stone-toothed edge. High above the street's elegant gables, stars appear.

His wife reaches over, turns the bottle, reads the label. A small smile. She knows her champagne. 'Nice,' she says.

Taking two flutes from the top cupboard, he chinks them onto the marble bench. He thinks of all the lies that came after that letter.

'You're off your game, Jackson. Anything wrong, son?' his father had said, early on, as they walked towards the last hole.

'What could be wrong?' he'd replied, slicing the ball.

But migraines pulsed in his head; his chest tightened into dangerous bands. When he blew the promotion two years in, he fell apart. Trapped and panicking, he told his wife everything. An evening like this, night coming, the vivid sharpness of it all.

There were no raised voices. They stayed together, under this roof, moving through these rooms. But he has not forgotten the way her fury seeped into the bones of the house; hung, waiting, in sunless corners. Even now, the clink of cutlery in a still room brings him almost to his knees.

When, years afterwards, a card was left for him at work, its message scratched in a teenage hand, he'd brought it to her like an offering. He'd watched, transfixed, gulping the air in small, grateful sobs as she singed it on the gas cooktop until it was a tight curl of black ash.

The foil comes clear of the bottle. She's watching him. There's a dry pop, the cork flying neatly through the half-opened window, landing out of view. It's dim, now, the air cooling. He pours both drinks, steals a glance at his wife. She looks light-headed already. Totting figures in her head, he thinks.

'Thank God that's over,' he says.

'About time.' She flicks her hair over a shoulder in that practised movement.

They sip in silence. Toasted cashew, a hint of citrus. A nice clean finish.

She touches his arm with a fingertip, says his name. She speaks of the cruise again. 'We could leave the boys behind. Imagine how nice it would be to get away.'

He doesn't answer. Lets her words circle in his mind.

In the garden, the automatic light flashes on, marking out a wide pool of yellow on the grass. They both look out, as if something unexpected might be there, waiting at the shadowy edge.

The sky is magnificent tonight: an arc of stars reaching towards the coast. A promising night.

Draining his glass, Jackson gives his wife a smile he knows she'll like. She drinks contentedly, taking the measure of the room with a triumphant tilt of her chin.

He looks outside, beyond the garden, the wall, the neat

enclave of roofs. He doesn't think of a cruise. He thinks of the rush of night air on his face, imagines a stretching road. A new car. Something faster. Something much, much smaller.

The Golden Hour

It was the last suggestion. *Bake your own bread.* Strange what you remember. The way he looks now reminds me of that time. There was a magazine article at the doctor's about fifty ways to save for a holiday. *You deserve it,* it told me. *Throw in extra seeds for a great pre-holiday boost!* But I didn't want a break, I needed to get away. There's a difference.

The bread making didn't last long. There was something depressing about those big blobs of dough, their slack-jawed shapes oozing onto the kitchen bench.

'Aren't you the real homemaker,' Eileen said, over the fence. 'I could smell the baking through my window.'

She was eyeing my washing as she spoke, a tickle of amusement on one side of her face. Her own clothes were turning on the line beside her, flapping brilliant white in the first hint of a breeze. Don't look at yours, Helen, I thought. She wants you to look at that tangle of stringy washing on your clothes hoist. Don't do it.

It was Brisbane's hottest summer in recorded history. Everything would be dry in an hour.

'It must be nice for Phillip,' Eileen prompted. 'Homemade bread. A little treat.' And she pulled her lips back into that knowing smirk. The look that always made me wonder how much more she'd learned at her open window. I stood with my hand on the dividing fence, listening to the rattle of Eileen's laundry trolley going back up the concrete path.

She's dead now. A lot has changed.

Phillip's got a doughy face. That's what reminded me of the bread. I can't imagine why I never noticed it so clearly, until today. It's the puffy face of a man fond of cakes and fried food, a man who could knock over a hamburger for morning tea and still have room for lunch. But Phillip's always been a modest eater. Partial to a scone, certainly – his mother baked them for her weekend visits.

'Sultana today, Phillip,' she'd sing out from the front door.

It was the only time he ever made tea.

'Oh, Helen, there you are,' his mother would exclaim, swivelling her doll's head to where I stood. 'Come and join us,' she'd say, as if this were her house, her table. 'You're very quiet today, Helen.'

Phillip would say nothing, just look at his mother and smile. There were times when he would not look at me at all. I usually stayed in the bedroom, folding the children's clothes or just staring into the backyard. A queasiness often ran through me as if I'd eaten too many scones instead of none at all.

A moderate, in many ways. That's how Phillip might be described. Plain meals, no alcohol, the weekly scone, maybe two, when his mother was alive. He took sandwiches to work.

'He's a good man, your Phillip,' people assured me, as if they could see depth beyond the stencilled edges of the person counting the fete takings or balancing the books for the scouts. A woman at the church once leaned across and whispered, 'He's got great faith, that fellow,' pointing at Phillip, not realising he was my husband. We both watched as he brought my best roses to the altar and arranged them with exquisite care.

I've still got the same clothes hoist, as it happens. I think it's the only one left in the street. A lot of the new people must have dryers these days, despite the Australian sun burning down just the same as it always did. There are even a couple of swimming pools along here now. The corner place has a cabana, whatever that is. Davina across the road told me.

'Everything's different now, Helen,' she said. 'Absolutely everything.'

I'll open up the house soon, hope for a cool evening breeze. It's been one of those still March days when you think the worst of summer is gone, then a great swoop of heat forces its way in. It's on afternoons like these – I might be gardening, or taking in the washing, not thinking of much at all except the creakiness coming into my shoulders – that I hear Phillip's words again. They slip into my mind the way a quiet person might enter a room. *If that shadow touches the side fence, I'll know you're guilty.*

Phillip was always looking for signs: a bird in a certain tree, rain on a feast day, the pattern of light across the house. For him, sin pressed itself into the landscape like a butter mould. When his words come back to me, I try to force them out. I hum show tunes. I used to sing hymns but that's gone. If I'm out the back, I make sure I don't look up at the dining-room window, don't sense a trace of my younger self there, rigid with fear, not knowing the reach of the sun, or what comes after its shadows.

I'm trying to recall, sitting here on the bed, how it came to this. Hopeful. I was certainly that, once. Patient. Loyal. Worried. I was all these things. Terrified. That, too. All these things but never at the same time. Each feeling was compressed, shaped by tiny degrees into a new form. Too slow to be noticed. Like pitch dropping.

I remember Marian telling me about an experiment at the university, years back, when she started doing mathematics. She was always such a clever girl, even when she was small. The department had set up a piece of tar – solid tar, hard enough to shatter – and waited for it to stir, to funnel itself into the narrow length of glass and drip into the beaker below. It had taken years for that pitch to form its first drop. And in the end, no one saw it fall. One morning, when they went in, there it was: a little lump of black pitch in the bottom of the jar.

'I'd love to see that,' I told Marian, back then.

'Oh, Mum, that's the point. You don't see it, it's so slow,' she said, not realising that it was the glossy mound, finally broken away, that I wanted to look at. Marian promised to take me to the university sometime. There've been eight more drops since then. She works there now, investigating something to do with statistics. I'll ring her later, when this day is over. I'll ring her brother, too.

Joey. He prefers being called that. Always has. 'I'm just walking up the road to pick up Joey from the party,' I told Phillip one day. That's how it started, the worst of it. Phillip stared as if he'd just swallowed the hard lump of the name and was waiting for it to settle. He stood up. 'He's not called Joey,' he said. I could feel his breath on my forehead, on the top of my head. 'How dare you call him Joey.' He laboured every syllable. 'He is Joseph. Nothing less. Nothing else. Do you understand?'

After that, it was always dangerous when the children weren't there. When he brought out the candles, especially. Even now, I won't have one in the house. Sometimes, when I see a crowded table of them in a shop, I have to steady myself, wait for the tremor to pass.

One night, Phillip got out the big wooden box where we kept the Christmas decorations. He started setting out candles on the table. Church candles. There were no decorations; I never did find the old Christmas ones. Then he took out pictures of the saints, laid them in tight rows. There were statues: little fluorescent ones, some of lurid plastic, an old one made of ivory with dark recesses of grime in the sleeves. There was a large statue of Saint Joseph, smiling fondly into the table, a piece of the tableau clearly broken away. Phillip set it at the top.

'Kneel down, you blaspheming whore,' he said to me.

Everything's different now, Helen. I wonder if that's true. Most mornings I hear the click, click of my neighbour's shoes as she walks to the train. How she bears working all day in those stiletto heels is a mystery. She's about Marian's age. Same confident step. I watch her making her way along the footpath and she looks perfectly fine. If I'm trimming the roses at the front, early, she'll nod or smile. I know her name. I've heard her husband calling out to her. 'Cathy, do you want a coffee?' I don't call her by her name. There are protocols. She has not introduced herself. It's that kind of neighbourhood now.

But I think about her sometimes. How can I know that everything in her life, behind the same biscuit-coloured brick, is normal? And how could I possibly judge? I have never done a day's paid work in my life. I am a mother. A wife. I have a chipped tailbone that still gives me pain, a slight limp that nobody notices. I cannot wear high heels. All the old bruises are there, hidden, unhealed. I have no religion at all.

Joey loves his job driving an ambulance, up on the coast. He likes surfing, and looking after people. He talks to me about hospital life, about the way patients are when they're in pain, when they're scared. I like hearing about all the medical conditions. Mostly, we speak on the phone. He doesn't like coming back to the house. He has long ago stopped asking me to leave his father. In recent years, I've stopped thinking of it myself.

I'm ready now, to make the call. I feel sure of everything. Joey has talked about the golden hour, the sixty precious minutes, the crucial time to act. I remembered that. And it's passed very quickly. I've spent it walking around the house. Sitting at the table, which is still pocked, in places, with candle burns. Thinking of Joey and Marian stuttering out their evening prayers, tears running down their cheeks, Phillip breathing hard into their faces. He was greedy for more words, more piety. We were all guilty.

In the hall, I recalled once hesitating in that air-locked space, feeling the ridges of the bronze and cream wallpaper, its thin pelt of flocked leaves comforting, somehow. A body can ricochet along a hall's length and stay standing, for a time.

Mostly, I've waited here, in the bedroom. The little clock my grandmother gave me chimes each fifteen-minute interval with a single fairy-bell note. I've been trying not to remember too much all at once. Through the window, I can see my new vegetable garden along the side fence. The freshly turned earth surprises me with its rich, opened-up colour.

Phillip is on the toilet.

'Helen! Come quickly!' Those were his words. He was shouting for help, but no one else could hear him. He kept gasping for air, but then his breath became so faint, so choked, that it was hardly more than a whisper. Like a prayer. I could see he was in agony. That's when I sat on the edge of the bed, where I could watch him.

Just once, he lifted his head and looked straight at me. I did not look away.

I waited. The clock sounded. Such a dainty bell. I've always liked it. Soon, another chime. When the third one came it seemed to ring out in the room, louder than before. By then, there were no other sounds. That's when I stood up, pressed my skirt flat with my hands. I resisted the urge to look in the dressing-table mirror. This is the moment, Helen, I said to myself. The pitch dropping. And no one will see it.

Phillip's body seems to take up most of the cubicle. This house was one of the first in the area to have a bathroom ensuite. How pleased I was when I first saw it. In truth, it's a modest sort of affair – a rather silly powder-pink that, at the start, seemed cheerful and fresh.

There's a phone on Phillip's side of the bed. The receiver feels cool in my hand. I see that Phillip's skin colour has changed, surprisingly quickly. So white. Joey mentioned that happens. *Pallor mortis*, he called it. Pallor. Phillip's mother used to use that word. 'Are the children getting enough to eat, Helen?' she'd say. 'Their pallor doesn't seem right.' And she'd look at me with that glittery certainty in her eyes. 'I'll bring over one of my casseroles. That's what I'll do.' And Phillip would say, 'Wonderful. That would be wonderful.'

His jaw has slackened. His eyes are open but I know he can't see me anymore. His underpants are tangled around his feet.

I dial. It's good to recognise the voice on the other end; she trained with Joey.

'This is Helen Coonan,' I tell her. 'It's my husband. I think it's his heart. I've just come in from the garden and found him. He's not moving. Not breathing. Come quickly.'

Death of a Friend

When she met her gaze, that last time, she remembered the mouse. Once, standing on the back verandah, night sunk deep into the trees, she'd heard the sound of bird's wings, wheeling close.

She knew it was the owl; she'd seen it, days before, perched on the sheeny muscle of ghost gum, turning its domed head.

But this time, she could see nothing.

There was only the lethal fold of feathers, swooping down, close to the grass. Then, a tiny creature carried aloft, shrieking from its miniature lungs, the shape of its outrage borne away, beyond a pitiless moon.

New Skins

Des ran his hand over the triangular shape of the dog's skull. 'It's nothing,' he told the boy. 'Her leg'll be fine. Just a small cut.'

The greyhound limped to the corner and scratched at the blanket lying there, making a mound of the pink-checked cloth and flopping down onto it. She stared at them with doleful eyes.

'Clumsiest damn dog ever born,' Des said.

The dog rested her long snout on her front paws. After a few minutes, she turned and licked at her wounded leg with delicate movements. 'Don't be upset, young Vincent,' Des said, tousling the boy's hair. 'They've got very thin skin. It's just a flesh wound.'

'Will April die?' Vincent said, standing in the doorway of the shed.

'Die! Not a chance,' Des said. 'I'm stuck with that old bag of bones. She's very tough.' He gave the boy a gentle poke in the shoulder. 'Tougher than you. Maybe even tougher than me.'

'Not tougher than my dad,' Vincent said. He puffed out his bony chest.

Des began picking up his tools, hooking them on a dusty pegboard above his workbench. He turned back to the boy, taking in the oversized t-shirt, the defiant set of the kid's jaw. He was growing tall, for sure, but still as thin as that fool dog in the corner.

'You're right there, son,' Des said. He couldn't keep a trace of sadness out of his voice. 'No one in the world tougher than your dad.'

The boy seemed satisfied. 'Can I walk April with you tomorrow?'

'If you like. When are you back at school?'

'Next week, I think.'

'Alright, after breakfast tomorrow, then. And don't be too early. I'm old. I need my sleep.'

'Okay. See you tomorrow.'

'You will. Behave yourself.'

Vincent waved back at the dog. 'Bye, April.'

Seconds later, Des heard the small creak of Vincent's front gate, the metallic slap of their screen door. 'Mum, I'm home,' he heard Vincent call out.

He heard no reply.

'Why did you get chickens?' Vincent squatted on the grass, fascinated by the black hens.

Des looked over at the boy. 'Rosemary wanted them. We've had them before. The fresh eggs are nice.'

'I hate eggs,' Vincent said. A curious hen was pecking close by. 'Does April try to catch them?'

Des hammered the final piece of wire onto the frame of the chicken coop. 'Nah, she's too lazy to chase anything these days.'

'What happened to the chickens you had before?'

'That was years ago. Before you came here.' The dog was padding towards them. 'Look, here's April, coming to see you.'

'Did they die?'

'What? The chickens? Yes, they died.'

'How?'

Des exhaled heavily. 'And how did I know you were going to ask me that?' He pulled another nail from the leather pouch tied around his hips. 'They got some sort of illness. It was a long time ago.'

Vincent held his hand out to the dog. 'Hi, April.'

The dog sniffed at a smear of mud on the boy's arm. To Des' surprise, Vincent snaked his arm around the dog's neck and kissed her grey coat.

'Doesn't your mum need you at home, young Vincent Daley?' Des was testing the strength of the coop with his broad hand. 'She might need you to do some jobs.'

'No. She's fine. She's in her room. I think she's asleep.'

'Asleep? Really? She must be tired. It's nearly ten o'clock in the morning.'

Rosemary came to the back door. 'Do you want a milkshake, Vincent?'

Without a word, the boy pushed past the dog and raced towards her. The chickens scattered in alarm.

'Come inside, hungry fellow,' Rosemary said. 'You'll have to wash your hands, though.'

Their own screen door slapped shut. Des could hear Vincent talking happily to his wife.

He looked at the house next door. The guttering had drooped even further since last week's storm. He peered over the chest-high fence. The side garden was badly overgrown. The place looked tired. Des remembered when it was built. A good solid house, back then. A Greek guy from Melbourne did all the work himself. Wife left him just as he was putting the finishing touches to the place. Literally putting in the front gate, poor bastard. She was a nice enough girl, Des thought, but you could see she was flighty. Took off back to the city. There'd been renters ever since, the place looking sadder by the year. It'd always been an unlucky house.

Des picked up his tools.

Rolling up the excess wire, he wondered about Vincent's mother. He'd been sawing and hammering for hours; how could Cheryl have slept through that? There'd been no sound at all from next door. No movement. No TV or radio. And on a warm day, all the windows on their side shut tight.

Des stood at the kitchen window, drinking his last coffee before bed. Caffeine never kept him awake. He always marvelled at people insisting on decaf when it was barely noon. Des ate what he liked, drank what he liked. A coffee at ten, cheese at midnight; it made no difference. All his life he'd slept soundly. He knew he was lucky. Rosemary had tossed and turned every night since they'd married.

Des pushed back the curtain edge with one finger. 'Light on next door.'

Rosemary was drinking a glass of juice, reading the local newspaper.

'Maybe Vincent's still a bit scared of the dark. I saw that light on when I got up last night,' she said.

'What time was that?' Des looked back at her. She seemed very small, crouched over the page, tapping her fingers as she read.

'Which time are you talking about?' she said. They smiled at each other.

'Poor old thing,' Des said. 'Maybe you should try the pilates stuff that Katherine's doing.'

'I'm not doing bloody pilates at my age, Des.' Rosemary folded the paper and tossed it into the basket they kept for recycling. 'It must have been about three. That damn possum rolled onto the roof again. I came down and got a glass of water. Saw the light on then.'

Des drained his coffee. 'When's the last time you saw Cheryl Daley?'

'Cheryl? I don't know.' Rosemary pushed in her chair. 'God, it's eleven o'clock already.'

They put the last of the things in the dishwasher.

'I'm serious, Rosie. When's the last time you saw her?'

'Not sure. April in the shed?'

'Yep. You know, I haven't seen Cheryl for days,' Des said. 'Maybe weeks. And I haven't heard a sound from the place. The only time I hear the gate, or their front door, I know it's Vincent, heading back from here.'

Rosemary shut the dishwasher, tilted her head in thought. 'I heard the television yesterday afternoon.'

'That was Vincent. I heard it go on when he left me, after April cut her leg.'

Rosemary looked through the glass panel of the back door, out into the darkness. 'Hmm. I haven't seen any washing on the line the last few days.'

'Maybe you should go over there tomorrow.'

Rosemary bit her lip. 'Maybe I should. But she's so odd, Des. She might not even come to the door. You know what she's been like since Teddy died.'

Des snorted. 'Hasn't changed much, far as I can see. Always a bit of a weirdo. Looks at me like I'm some sort of maniac.'

Rosemary pushed the pedal bin against the wall with her foot. 'A discerning woman, clearly.'

'Hilarious. Seriously, she goes out of her way to avoid me. A few weeks ago I was digging in that garden bed near the mailbox and she pulled up outside her place. When she saw me she drove away again.'

'I'm sure she just remembered something,' Rosemary said, following Des into the hall. 'They've always kept to themselves.'

The light from next door, coming through the narrow side window, made it easy to see in the darkness. Des kicked off his shoes at the bottom of the stairs. 'I don't think she's there, Rosie. I'm serious. I think that kid's there on his own.'

Rosemary looked at the patch of light on the hall carpet. 'Des, that's just crazy. He's nine years old.'

'Well, we'll see. Let's find out tomorrow.'

Rosemary was instantly awake. She heard a second thump on the roof, not as heavy as the first. Possums. Two now, by the sound of it. One was already rolling from the grevillea to the gutter on the other side of the house.

She looked around, her eyes adjusting to the shapes of her bedroom furniture, just visible in the moonlight. The silver charms she'd seen in town yesterday came into her mind. A whole row of them, hanging on long chains in the window at Gleeson's. There'd been a choice of a possum, an echidna or a platypus. A platypus! Surely the ugliest animal on earth, Rosemary thought. She'd seen one at her aunt's place up in Queensland when she was a girl. A slick, freaky-looking creature just below the surface of the creek. Maybe tourists buy those necklaces, she thought, trying to get comfortable. But there are hardly any tourists around here. Not really much to see. There's the lake, but mainly locals use that. The boating crowd on the weekend, the swimming club, the odd fisherman. Rosemary pulled the covers around her shoulders. And ghosts, she thought.

Rosemary hadn't noticed the Gleeson girl yesterday, standing behind the counter in her parents' jewellery shop. Not at first. It was her hair that had caught Rosemary's attention as she stood on the footpath, looking in. She saw a flick of yellowy curls, sent tumbling down the back of a tight grey dress. And there she was, her face reflected in the shop's large gilt mirror. Ellie Gleeson. Back in town again.

Rosemary had been at the doctor's, about five doors up. She'd stopped to stare at the cushioned pads of rings, the rows of pendants. She had no interest in jewellery. Ellie was in the far corner of the shop, admiring her own reflection. There was no one else inside. She looked so much more grown-up, Rosemary thought. Amazing the difference a few years makes at that age. She'd watched Ellie pluck at her hair, check her lipstick, put a finger to a heavy gold choker around her neck. From the back, she resembled an athletic mermaid. Fitting, somehow. There was always something a bit eerie about her. The girl from the lake. The girl who lived.

Ellie seemed to sense that someone was looking at her. She spun around quickly, meeting Rosemary's eyes through the glass. Feeling spooked by her hard stare, Rosemary had put her head down and made for the car.

Rosemary felt wide awake now. She knew she'd have to go downstairs. She wasn't thirsty, but long years of insomnia had taught her to just go with it: get up, have a few sips of water, try to settle again. Sometimes, this worked.

She didn't bother turning on the lamp. As she headed towards the stairs, she glanced out the front window where the bedroom curtains didn't quite meet. The moon was shining on the lemon-scented gums across the road. In the past few days, the trees had shucked off the last of their old bark. Their new skins shone grey-white, regal and beautiful, their full, dark heads almost invisible against the ploughed field behind them.

A small movement caught her eye, down at road level. Something red, moving in the dark. She went back to her bedside table to get her glasses. Des, mumbling in his sleep, rolled towards the wall. By the time she got back to the window, the road seemed deserted. Then she saw it. Someone stealing Cheryl's old Datsun. Someone in the driver's seat. Small. Too small. It looked like a child. It was. Vincent in a red t-shirt.

Rosemary looked at her bedside clock. It was almost three o'clock in the morning.

'You should have gone down to him, Rosie,' Des said, sipping his breakfast coffee from a large earthenware mug.

'I didn't want to scare him, wandering around in my nightie. I thought Cheryl might have asked him to get something. I would have looked a fool then, wouldn't I?'

Des crunched his toast. 'Did you see the mysterious Cheryl?'

Rosemary shook her head.

'Thought not. Especially not in the dead of night,' Des

said, taking a second, triumphant bite. 'Though nothing would surprise me.'

'Look, I came down for some water and when I got back upstairs, he was gone. Simple as that. As far as I could tell their house was in complete darkness. It was weird.'

Rosemary went to let April out of the shed. The dog soon appeared at the back door.

'G'day, girl,' Des said, patting her head as she came to his side. Her long tail beat against the chair leg. 'What was he doing in the car, anyway?'

Rosemary was looking down the back garden, distracted. 'I don't know, Des. He was sort of messing about as far as I could see. He was holding the steering wheel. The boot was open as well. It was pretty bright; I could see him fairly clearly.'

She leaned against the kitchen bench, a teacup in one hand. 'You know, it looked for all the world like he was pretending to drive.'

'Little bugger. Maybe that's exactly what he was doing.'

'At three o'clock in the morning?'

Des slipped a corner of buttery toast into the dog's mouth. 'Pretty strange, I grant you.'

'I wish you wouldn't do that,' Rosemary said. 'You've ruined that silly dog.'

'True enough,' Des said, scratching behind the dog's ears as she chewed noisily, strings of saliva dribbling from her jaw.

'I think I'll go over there today, Des. Talk to Cheryl.'

'Then you'll get the boy into trouble. He's coming over

here soon. Why don't we see how the land lies then.' Des stood up. 'C'mon, April. Out with you. Let's have a look at those chooks.'

Des glanced over at the Daley house as he walked down the garden. There were no windows open.

Rosemary was standing in the back doorway. She still had her town clothes on. 'Has Vincent gone home already?' she said, putting her bag on the kitchen bench.

Des was digging in the vegetable patch. 'No sign of him. Didn't come over.'

'Really? That's unusual. Did you call out for him?'

'Yep. Nothing. Even knocked on the front door. Not a sound. No one there.' Des straightened up and stuck the spade into the soil. 'Don't know why we can't just buy our veggies like normal people.' He looked at Rosemary. 'How did you get on at the doc's again?'

Rosemary turned towards the kitchen. 'Yes, fine. Nothing to worry about. I'm making tea. Where's the dog?'

Des wiped his hands on his trousers. His back was sore, low down. 'Last time I saw her she was inside, lying on your good rug.'

Rosemary shook her head. 'Des, I rue the day that blasted dog appeared in our front garden. I really do.'

'I seem to remember you were the one who threw her the last of your ham sandwich, my dear. Only reason she hung around.' Des looked up, smiling. Rosemary was staring at the house next door. 'What's wrong?'

She was pointing at the Daleys' frosted bathroom window. She beckoned to Des to come closer. 'I just saw someone's head move across that window,' she whispered. 'There's definitely someone in there.'

Des squinted back at the house. He couldn't see anything. 'Do you think it's Vincent?'

'Don't know. Looked too big. Let's go inside,' she whispered.

'Des, do you think we should call the police?'

The final credits were rolling on the TV. Rosemary pressed the remote. It suddenly seemed very quiet.

'I don't know, Rosie. What do we say? We saw a kid in his own house. We saw a kid in his own car? The mother had a sleep-in? Not much of a rap sheet, is it?' Des took a gulp of beer from the bottle. 'When does school start back?'

'Tomorrow. I met Thelma Switzer in the street yesterday. She had her grandchildren with her. "The fun's all over," she told them. "Hard work starts on Monday." No wonder the poor kids looked crestfallen.'

'Can't imagine anyone having fun with Thelma Switzer, no matter what the time of year.' Des drained his bottle. 'Okay, first thing tomorrow, we're out in the front garden. We'll stay there until someone appears.'

'I saw Ellie Gleeson in the jeweller's yesterday,' Rosemary said.

'Really? Jeez, haven't seen her for a while. Back in town, eh? What did she look like?'

'Fine. Quite beautiful, actually. Her hair's very long.' Rosemary turned her empty wineglass on the table beside her. 'I suppose she'd be into her twenties by now. She's a bit spooky, isn't she?'

Des snorted. 'You'd look spooky, too, if you killed your two best friends.'

'She didn't kill anyone, Des. It was an accident, for God's sake. They drowned.'

'Her idea to take the boat out. Bloody stupid in that weather. And what about poor Teddy Daley? Just minding his own business, bunking off, doing a bit of fishing. Poor bastard dies trying to save her scrawny neck.' Des was tapping the empty beer bottle lightly on his knee. 'And there's young Vincent next door, with no father. And Cheryl, nutty as she is, there on her own. Not even a body to bury.' Des turned to look at his wife. 'Are you going to sleep after that wine?'

'I only had a drop. Hope so.' Rosemary seemed distracted.

'You okay?' Des said. He felt a small shiver of fear that he could not account for.

Rosemary picked up her empty glass. 'Me? Yes, I'm fine. Do you think Cheryl got some sort of pay-out after Teddy died? There was talk of it in town.'

'Doubt it,' Des said. 'First thing she would have done was trade in that old wreck of a Datsun.' He stretched and stood up. 'Look, Rosie, we can't worry about the dead. We have to worry about the living. Speaking of which, how's Katherine?'

Rosemary brightened. 'Good. She's booked the waterbirth unit.'

'The what?'

'Waterbirth unit. Where she'll have the baby. She's having a doula, too.'

Des looked down at his wife. 'Are you going to tell me, or make me ask?'

Rosemary laughed. 'It's like a midwife. It's an ancient practice.'

She stood up beside him. She's lost weight, Des thought, with sudden clarity. 'I don't want any ancient practices for my future grandson,' he said. He was looking intently at Rosemary, trying to work out what was different about her. 'I want modern medicine. I want an heir. I want a dynasty.'

Rosemary smiled. 'You're a bit late for all that, Des. Katherine's nearly forty now. And there's no way they'll move back here so you can forget those wild fantasies of yours about building a family compound.'

They both moved towards the stairs.

'Anyway,' Rosemary said, 'who said it's going to be a boy?'

Des grinned in the semi-darkness. 'I did. I can be a bit spooky, too, you know.'

Des was snoring within minutes. Watching his chest rise and fall, Rosemary wondered whether she'd have been less of an insomniac if she'd spent forty-two years lying beside a quiet sleeper. She doubted it.

The possums hadn't arrived. There'd been no familiar drum roll as they careered across the metal roof. Perhaps hit by a car. She often saw their smashed carcasses lying in the road at the front of their house, their sweet, pointed faces drying in the sun.

She sat up. Her hand moved automatically to her left breast. Through the cotton of her nightdress she could feel the hard lump down low on one side. She'd have to tell Des soon. She'd seen how he'd looked at her this evening; he knew something wasn't right. Katherine had insisted she could stay with her after the surgery. For one breathless moment, Rosemary wondered whether she'd live to see her grandchild. She got out of bed, told herself to stop being so ridiculous. It's not like the old days, she thought. Not like her mother. Best she didn't think about it too much.

She looked out at the gums across the road. Eleven. She remembered the first time she'd stood at the window, wide awake in the middle of the night, counting them. Their quiet beauty always calmed her. It wasn't as bright tonight but there they were, softly illuminated in the velvety darkness.

There was a small screech of metal. Rosemary knew it, instantly. The catch on the side gate. Three ragged scrapes and a high creak as it opened. Her heart pounded. She was turning to wake Des when she realised who it must be. Vincent. His hands had never quite mastered the sticky latch, and he always made a distinctive sound as he tried to get it open. She looked back at Des. He had one arm crossed over his chest. He was in a deep sleep.

What on earth was Vincent up to now? She put her glasses on and stole downstairs in the dark. By the time she reached the kitchen, the door of the back shed was standing open. Even though she was sure it must be Vincent out there, she felt adrenaline sweep through her. She stood near the sink window, shielded by folds of short curtain. April appeared from the shed, snuffling at the ground, puzzled and excited by the nocturnal activity.

Seconds later, the boy came into view, grabbing at the dog's collar before she ran out of reach. He would have known that April wouldn't bark.

'April!' he called out, before remembering to whisper. 'April. Come here, girl.'

The dog turned back and nuzzled against Vincent's hip. The boy sat down on the low stone wall and put his arm around her. Neither moved. They were just metres from Rosemary as she stood in the dark, the curtain moving slightly in the open window.

She watched Vincent push his face into the dog's neck. Rosemary squinted into the darkness, wondering what he was doing.

'Goodbye, girl,' he said.

He was crying. Rosemary could see his thin shoulders rising and falling with each sob. Goodbye? Where was he going?

The dog stood patiently, staring into the back garden, making no attempt to escape Vincent's chokehold.

'You're the best girl ever,' Vincent said. He kissed the dog's grey coat.

Rosemary could just make out April's thin legs, the slow wag of her tail back and forth. She suddenly felt a surge of affection for the dog, more than any other animal she'd ever owned. She blinked back tears. Surely Cheryl wasn't going to disappear in the middle of the night? And why? Rosemary wished she'd woken Des. She could see that Vincent was fully dressed. He had his prized football shirt on, the white number nine glowing faintly in the dark.

The boy led the dog back into the shed. Sniffing loudly, he closed the door. 'Good girl,' he said softly, through the wood. 'See you, April.'

He sounded so young. When he turned his face towards the kitchen window Rosemary was certain he'd seen her, but he wiped his nose on the back of his hand and disappeared down the side of the house. She heard the gate close; a single clink as the latch fell into place.

Rosemary's heart began to race. She moved through the dark hall to the front of the house and stood in the shadows, looking into the street. She saw nothing. Cheryl's Datsun hadn't moved. A couple of crows cawed to each other further down the road. No traffic. She knew it was very late.

She sat down in the chair just inside the window, pushing it deeper into the unlit room. Vincent must be running away, she thought. Katherine did that once, when she was about the same age. It was six hours before they found her, crouched on the back steps of the Jacksons' place, drawing pictures in the dirt with a long stick. They were terrified she'd gone as far as the lake. From that day, Rosemary had never had a full night's sleep again.

Sitting stiffly in the chair, Rosemary rubbed her arms in agitation. If Cheryl couldn't be bothered looking after her son, she was going to do it. She'd keep watch over the Daleys' front gate for the whole night, if necessary. The mere thought of Vincent trying to drive was preposterous, but he was tall for his age. It wasn't impossible. And he loved cars. Before the accident, she'd often seen Teddy working on the Datsun, Vincent by his side handing up tools and talking non-stop. Poor little fellow, Rosemary thought. He's been lost since his father died. Cheryl and the boy cooped up in that house. Once the police stopped calling, and those rude media people had finally gone away, Rosemary couldn't remember seeing a single visitor come to their door.

She thought back to when the Daleys first arrived, pulling up in that same car, the side windows covered with bags and boxes. Vincent must have been about five. She remembered how he'd raced into the back garden. How she'd thought he was a girl, at first, because his hair was quite long. Rosemary had introduced herself to his parents. It'd been awkward. They didn't give their names; she'd had to ask them. She'd offered them the small box of plant cuttings that she was about to put into her own garden. They'd stared at them as if they were poisonous, Teddy taking them reluctantly with his free hand.

When she'd asked where they were from, Teddy had said, 'Queensland.' Nothing more. Cheryl had stood, silent and unsmiling, plucking at her sleeves with nervous hands. 'Near Emerald,' Teddy told her when Rosemary pressed him further. She still remembered the strange look that crossed his face when she told him she'd spent half her childhood out that way. 'Never liked the place much,' he said, before making an excuse and going inside. Days later, she saw that her cuttings had drooped and died near their front door, still in their shallow cardboard box.

Rosemary smoothed the armrests of the chair. She realised that she knew almost nothing about the Daleys. Even Vincent, at his young age, seemed adept at revealing no details about the family. They'd simply arrived and unpacked to a quiet, hidden life, letting the shrubs and trees between the two houses grow unchecked, closing across their roof like the wing of a giant bird.

And then, the storm.

'I felt him grip my arm,' Ellie Gleeson told the inquest, her voice shaking. 'He was holding me up in the water. He pushed me forward, yelled at me to swim for the jetty. I could see some headlights on the shore, and the flashing blue of the police lights. Everything else was swirling grey.'

Half the town had sat motionless in the stifling air of the old courthouse, listening to Ellie's testimony. The storm had barrelled across the lake, she said, the rain pelting down, sharp as pins. She'd never heard wind so loud. The afternoon turned dark in moments. 'It was like a tornado,' she said. After the boat tipped, she told the hushed room, she'd never seen her friends again. 'Not alive, I mean,' Ellie said, staring around the room with a bewildered, frantic face. Rosemary recalled the Lennox girl's mother, inconsolable in her loss, collapsing in the heat and being helped outside, sagging between two grim-faced sons.

Ellie Gleeson had been the last to see Teddy Daley. 'I didn't look back, after that,' she said. 'I didn't see what happened to him. I just kept going. I didn't think the lake could ever be that rough … I thought I was going to die.' Dabbing a ball of damp tissue into each eye, she told the court what she'd seen: the back of Teddy Daley's head, sinking under the churning water.

Rosemary was beginning to feel chilly, but she didn't dare move from the window. She was sure the car keys were on the table in the hall. If Vincent had some mad idea about driving, she'd go after him, never mind that she was in her nightie.

She thought about the last time she'd seen Cheryl. At the mailbox, about a fortnight ago, she'd spotted her standing inside her front window, staring through the venetian blinds. She was smoking. Rosemary had lifted the fan of mail in her hand in salute, but Cheryl had reached up and tilted the blinds, leaving a small wreath of smoke clinging, momentarily, to the glass. Rosemary had wondered then, not for the first time, whether there was a past, whether she was hiding from something. Or someone.

The old blue upholstered chair felt very comfortable. I don't sit here nearly often enough, Rosemary decided. She was amazed to find that she could hear Des snoring in the room above her. She envied him, the way he just turned off. Sometimes, she'd barely finish the page of a book and he'd be gone. That might change, she thought, and a wave of sadness swept over her.

She stared into the street. Nothing. Two cars passed, one going far too quickly. Silence. She was going to sit here all night, she decided, watching out for Vincent. And in the morning, after breakfast, she was going to tell Des about the cancer. Let him sleep for now. She was tired herself.

The Daleys' gate creaked. Rosemary started, amazed to find that she'd dozed off. For a moment, she didn't know where she was. Then she saw the window, the trees across from her, the night sky, cloudier than before. There was someone in the Daleys' front garden.

Rosemary stood up, keeping back from the window. A man. A man with a suitcase in one hand, a bag in the other, both heavy. He slid them into the back of the Datsun, alongside other boxes already stacked against the seat. Rosemary peered at the house. As far as she could tell, there were no lights on.

Cheryl appeared. So, Rosemary thought, another man. Well, good for her. Why did she have to be so weird about it? Cheryl had her hair scraped back into a tight ponytail. She was also carrying bags, two soft hold-alls, clearly full.

She heaved them into the back with the others. She did not look at the man, or speak to him. They each made a number of trips between the house and the car, passing each other on the path like phantoms. Still no lights. Rosemary was suddenly chilled by the thought that the windows might have been blacked out in some way.

The old Datsun, weighed down with luggage, hunkered low on the road as if reluctant to go anywhere.

The man appeared again, carrying a duvet and a bare pillow, which he stuffed into the back seat, making a little nest beside the bags. Cheryl came out, pulling up the hood of a dark top. She went straight to the car and sat in the passenger seat without closing the door. She kept her hand on top of a small, square bag in her lap, as if it were a restless lapdog.

And there was Vincent, walking towards the car. He was moving slowly, a patterned bag stuffed under one arm. Just as he went to climb in, he dropped the bag and ran towards Rosemary, stopping in their front garden.

'Vinnie!' she heard the man hiss.

The boy was standing in Rosemary's driveway, looking down into the darkness towards the back. She couldn't see his face clearly, but he gave a childish wave into the night air. Waving to the dog, Rosemary thought. She felt sure, then, that she would never see Vincent again.

The man walked over to the boy, holding a finger to his lips. He was thin, fit-looking. He had a close-cropped beard. He put his hand on Vincent's shoulder. As they both turned towards the car, the moonlight passed across their faces. She could see the terrible resignation in Vincent's face. As she watched them go, she realised that she knew them both. Bracing herself against the wall with one hand, her nerves singing along her arm, up her spine, across her open mouth, she was certain that she knew the man. It was Teddy Daley.

Rosemary's breathing was so loud she was sure they would all hear her. She wanted to shout out to Des, but she did not move.

Teddy shepherded Vincent into the car. Cheryl stared ahead into the road.

'Hop in, quick, Vinnie. Mind your head.' Rosemary clearly heard him say it. She recognised his voice. There was no mistake.

Rosemary watched, her heart pounding in her chest, as Vincent curled into the nest of bedding while his father clipped the seatbelt around him. Teddy Daley. Alive. As she steadied herself, feeling suddenly nauseous, she wondered how a young boy might survive a lie this big. How it might be explained away. Why it had to be done.

Even Des might have woken if they'd started the Datsun. They were careful. Rosemary heard only the crack and pop of small stones as they let the car roll slowly towards the dip in the road just beyond their house. She waited, listening for the engine, heard the car sputter into life. She pushed aside the curtain, knowing that she would soon see its headlights as it climbed away from Burchardt

Creek, past the old woolshed, the turn-off for the lake, the Gleesons' big place on the hill, the road straightening towards the highway.

Rosemary pulled the curtains together, even though the first mauve light of the day seemed close. She would tell Des today. Tell him about the cancer, and the surgery. It would be hard for a while, she'd explain, but she would be fine. Just fine.

Rosemary let herself out the front door. She felt a slight chill on her bare arms. She stood in the driveway, just where Vincent had stood, where he'd waved in the dark to the dog he loved. There was a little more light. Dawn was certainly coming.

She vowed then, looking at the abandoned house next door, the sagging guttering on that side, that she would never tell a soul that Teddy Daley was alive. That for reasons she would never know, he had taken his chance when it came, swum away into the safety of oblivion. That whatever he'd done, a small boy needed him.

Rosemary looked over at the gum trees, their white trunks solid as ancient columns, their tight new skins waiting for the day.

Tying the Boats

A week after she married him, she cut her hair. The scissors made a hungry sound working their way through the curls.

'You cut your hair, Eve,' he said, when he came home. Nothing more.

She thought he might have said, 'You cut off your beautiful hair,' but his mouth could not make the shape of beautiful, even then.

She kept the hair in a drawer. A great hank of it, bound together in two places with ribbon almost the same dark red. Sometimes, when she was searching in the big oak chest that she brought from home, she'd see it stretched against the back of the drawer, flattened into the joinery like a sleek, cowering animal.

Once, she lifted it out, held it up to the light to catch the last of its fading lustre. She weighed it in her hands. The hair was thick, substantial, heavy as the ropes they'd used when she was a girl, tying the boats when storms were coming.

The New Bride

We have arrived. Two couples in a white Citroën, nosing gracelessly into the last parking space. There's silence at last after the rattle of the engine, the eternal meanderings of jazz. The smell of leather polish still clings to everything, swirls around me in the back of the car, in the pit of my stomach. In front, my father-in-law continues to clutch the wheel with both hands. It has been a long day.

'The old hotel,' he says, into the windscreen. There's relief in his voice; the weekend in France has been his idea. He turns to his wife. 'A good run, in the end, Caroline.'

She refolds her hands in her lap. 'I suppose so,' she says, without turning her head. 'I hope we're going to get dinner, David.'

I watch the slope of her shoulders, the careful sweep of ash-blonde hair curling in at the nape. We all stare ahead at the car park's encircling wall. Here and there, excess mortar hangs from its yellow bricks in congealed drops. I glance across at my husband, who is squeezing the edge of the seat as if we're cornering too fast.

Across the square, the hotel looks crowded. Beyond urns of flowering shrubs, there are people at every window. In the dining room, a woman peers out, points to the spinal curve of the church roof nearby. A man at the hotel door, dressed in holiday stripes, tilts his head back and laughs. The cobblestone lanes are fading in the evening light. I wind down the window, take a few breaths of mountain air. I do not want to be here. Not in this car, in this town, hostage to a language we all speak with a nailed tongue. Here, with these strangers.

My father-in-law says he'll go and check in, find out about dinner. 'Stay in the car,' he says. 'I'll sort it out.' A mistake. He loves the place but his tongue has the biggest nail and his temper is quick. Since the heart problems, he could blow at any time.

We wait. A jet pushes through the clouds above us. A dog yaps briefly on the other side of the wall and is scolded into silence. Glass clinks into a bin. David does not reappear.

The delay crushes the car. I wonder what might come after this morning's rolling ferry, after miles of tall forests flanking wrong roads. It's getting dark. Moths begin circling the street lamps, smacking their papery skulls on the metal shades.

'Go and see what's happening, Paul, for heaven's sake,' Caroline says.

My husband pushes the car door open. He carries a dozen good summers spent in these hills, a throwback geniality bundled in his heart. He is all our best hopes.

122

But he walks towards the hotel with a wary step, as if the flagstones might be mined. Under the lintel, he hesitates, bows his head, vanishes.

We're alone now. Two women joined in marriage: the mother, the new wife. We're afraid of each other. There is nothing I can say that will soothe her heart, ease out the barb of forsaking a son, mend the fallacy of gaining a daughter.

'You know,' she says, her voice flaring in the silent car like unexpected lightning, 'we've come here every year since we married.' She looks straight ahead at the ancient wall. I can see her profile projected onto the side window, scrupulous as a mirror. 'I hate this place,' she says. Quiet but firm. 'I simply cannot stand it.'

Her shoulders droop, just for a moment, beneath pale peach cashmere. She does not seem to expect a reply.

I try to imagine the looping shape of forty years. This leather-bound car, this returned-to place. I picture the dim porticos of a thousand churches, bridges, monuments, studded into these hills. And now, perhaps, this final mortification: nowhere to lay out her bones, to let bitterness drain away in thin runnels. My fingers have closed around the door handle. I resist the urge to run into the hopeless blank of a country night.

Father and son are walking towards the car, their same-shaped mouths stretched into nervous smiles. A lost booking, they tell us, leaning on the car door. A conference of actuaries. Insurance, you know. No trace of our name.

But there's a second hotel, owned by the same family. Twins. Imagine! Everything's fine, they say, almost in unison, as if they've rehearsed it in the foyer.

David passes his wife a paper menu where someone has scratched a rough map in red pen. She glances at it, hands it back without a word.

The last of the light has gone. The car chugs into life again. Our headlights rake the dining room as we turn, picking out a family bending over their meals. A teenage girl looks up and watches us go with a blank, chewing face.

Out on the road, the hedges loom. I lean my head on the window, feel the frosty glass against my temple.

'We shouldn't be too late to get some dinner,' my father-in-law says, his hands on the wheel again, his mood rising. He puts the radio back on. Dancing music. The coiffed head beside him does not move.

'Hopefully not too late,' my husband says to me.

I watch the dark shapes as we pass by. Marvel at their height.

These Ordinary Nights

Tom's awake. Muffled footsteps on the carpet, a scrape of chair. He's walking over our heads, vampire bright. We don't look at each other, just keep watching the show, the flash and noise of it, that woman who won the car. 'I can't believe it, I can't believe it!' she yells, tears on her cheeks, the camera up close.

'That corner cabinet needs a polish, Susan,' Keith says, while the TV claps and claps. But I know he couldn't care less about dull wood. He's been looking over at the photo of Tom again. The smiling one. I should put it away.

'Goodnight, goodnight,' they're chorusing, balloons coming down.

'We'd best get up to bed, Susan,' Keith says, every night. He presses the button on the remote. Everything vanishes.

Upstairs, Tom's stirring his breakfast coffee in the corner of his room. We hear the spoon ringing in his cup, calling through the floor like a delicate bell. I'll collect the milk jug later, when he's gone.

In the kitchen, I set his tray by the microwave, leave a

meal thawing on the bench. Tom does love his shepherd's pie. He's always famished when he gets home, banging about in the first of the light.

We go on up, Keith just ahead, his hand gripping the banister the whole way. A blue glow chills the edge of Tom's door as we pass. I hear the click of his keyboard. The endless click.

'Goodnight, son,' we say, into the wood.

Click, click.

In our room, Keith whispers, 'Remember last Christmas, Susan? Remember when—'

And I say, 'Don't, please. Just don't.'

We lie together in pantomime sleep, picturing that day. Playing cards by the fire, the scent of pine in the room, all of us picking at the last of the cake. Tom appeared at the door, stepped in, leaned against the edge of the sofa. Gran said, 'You were always a great little player, Tom,' and she reached up, with her bracelet of tinsel, and proffered her glass of sherry. Tom bent down and sipped it, like a child. We all laughed in surprise – too high, too loud. I tried not to think of the roll of banknotes, fat as a cigar, that I'd seen the week before, poking from Tom's pocket. Keith smiled across at me, raised his glass. He's coming back to us, his eyes said.

We always hear Tom leave. The stones on the driveway are as small and white as milk teeth. We hear the crush of them. Sometimes, objection rises like a thing and presses its weight on the window, staring into the empty street below.

Sometimes fear sits on our bed. It scoops a hollow with its bulk that I cannot smooth away.

In the abandoned quiet, memories edge in. Keith in his pyjamas, shouting in the hall. 'What the hell are you up to, son? We need to know what's going on.' And the way he roared, 'This minute!' with his voice cracking, his cheeks flocked purple with rage.

And Tom standing there, his coat over his shoulder, no expression on his face. The way his answer came, slow-voiced, precise, his words silting into the carpet. 'If you don't like it, I'll leave for good. Then you'll never know where I am. Ever.'

And the way he didn't slam the door like a normal teenager, just shut it very softly. Click, click.

So, these nights — these ordinary nights — disquiet stretches across the bed, fatly tame. In the hush, there is only the slow rasping of unknown things, curling like an abrading tongue on how it came to be like this. And where, exactly, Tom goes in our car.

The Memory Bones

'Don't be afraid, Geraldine,' she said to me.

On land she had a lumbering style, yet her movements could still be delicate. Broad-hipped and big-eyed, she had come, in later life, to seem oddly like her jut-boned cows.

With two quick steps her knees were gone, then she lowered the rest of her body, her swimming mouth forming long before her torso felt the keen slap of water, unexpectedly cold. I wasn't sure whether the mimed 'ooh' of her lips signalled delight or disgust but she swam into the centre with easy movements, her arms pushing out rhythmically, her chin lifted high. She kept her sunhat on, tied down with strips from an old apron. The years of isolation had made my grandmother thrifty. As she swam away, its long ribbons trailed behind her like tame, floral eels.

The dam seemed vast but it was the smallest on the property, in the '200' paddock, close to the house. Two hundred acres of low blanched hills, tinted brown and dusty green. Walled by heat, static as a painting. The

French woman who came every Wednesday for cream and jars of relish would turn her sorrowing European eyes towards the bush.

'It is all so much the same,' she would murmur, as if seeing it for the first time. 'So faded.'

From the dam, we could not see the house, only its thread of woodsmoke lacing through the tallest of the trees. At the back of the old place the land dropped away sharply, past the dipping yards and down into a natural basin of clay and rock. Rain was never wasted here. It coursed along two slim gullies and pooled near a glade of bowing paperbarks. Years before, Mason, that patient old horse, shackled to what looked like a giant sugar scoop, had dragged great mounds of dirt up the slope and away. The water was deep, and permanent. Even in a hard summer, it never went dry. Its hugging wall of earth, and the drooping trees on the other side, cast broad arms of shade across the surface. If a sudden breeze lifted the tendrils from the water, it felt as if something other-worldly had stirred.

William, the oldest of my cousins, his shadow moustache mesmerising us all, had intoned in his half-man voice that the dam was bottomless. 'Be careful,' he'd said, his square face looming over us. 'You'll never be seen again if you go down too far.' The water was almost black, and it looked thick, as if you could catch it up and hold it in your hand like a curiosity.

My grandmother's wrapped head bobbed on the surface. I squatted on a flat rock, worrying about snakes. The last of the strong afternoon sun was sliding a burning finger along the parting of my hair. Soon, I would have to join her. Perhaps there was a snake beneath this rock, tilting its awful Martian head, listening, waiting. I was always worried about snakes, even at home, scared of what might be knotted into the old fig, the compost heap, the unreached end of my bed.

A little tide lapped heavily at my toes. I wondered what made the water so dark. Through the trees, a mob of cattle watched us. Without movement or expression, one animal lifted its tail in a single, hydraulic arc. Manure dropped to the ground with a loud splat. From my rocky perch above the water, the colour looked suspiciously similar.

My grandmother was calling me, sweeping her arms back and forth. She looked a little cold. I wanted to ask her whether she was treading water or just keeping warm. I wanted to know how deep it was. There was no choice. I had to go in. She was only swimming here to keep me happy.

I wasn't prepared for the bottom. My leg sprang upwards in horror. Not, after all, an infinite drowning pool, but hideous all the same. Not solid, not jagged on town-soft feet, but thick and spongy, almost warm. Like walking on a giant tongue. Better to swim, better to keep feet clear of what might lurk beneath.

My navy one-piece seemed flimsy armour. When I had modelled it for my mother, her mouth gently compressed, her eyes unreadable, the pin-spots and little cut-outs on the sides seemed stylish for town or country. Grown-up. But on that rock I'd seen small circles of my own chicken skin through the peepholes. A creature could get in there, wrap itself around me, pull me down to the unspeakable depths. This much I'd learned: you needed special togs for farms.

Today, we were the only two in the world. The men were long gone, moving out on horseback, looking distracted and important, off to check fences and move stock. The morning's housework was done. Great sails of washing flapped on the line. The dinner joint sat ready for the oven, daubed in lard and a thick dusting of black pepper, a veil of muslin draped across it like a bride. The old dog watching it with his yellow eyes would not hear the riders returning for many hours.

It was a delicious, still time. Our time. We talked and sipped tea in pretty cups. Sometimes, I'd lie in the sleep-out, thumbing through *Reader's Digest*s, shelved in their dozens behind an oil-cloth curtain. The afternoon sun shone through the window's brain-patterned glass, patching the chenille bedspread with stretched squares of pink and green.

'Would you like to go for a swim?' my grandmother had said, and I must have stared, because she made a tiny, musical chuckle in her throat. 'It won't exactly be what you're used to, but it will be nice. I used to like swimming when I was your age.'

We'd packed some sandwiches and lemon slice in dented tin boxes and walked together through the spiky grass. She chatted and asked me questions, her head turning occasionally towards the grey spire of mountain at the furthest edge of the property, where the men had gone.

There was a gunshot. One. We both jumped. Silence, then a single high-pitched whoop carried across the valley like a spear of sound. Her mouth shrank in disgust.

'It's nothing,' she said. 'Just the Courtneys.'

Beyond a wall of trees, a second trail of smoke rose in the distance. Neighbours. It came as a shock that there was anyone nearby.

'Just ignore it,' my grandmother said.

We moved on. I kept my head down, watching for a streak of black or killer brown, lowering each foot with infinite care, wary as a tightrope walker.

It was quiet at the dam. Just the sounds of the bush and the peaceful lap of water against the rocks. I'd finally pushed off and was swimming out towards her, feet well clear of the sucking clay.

'We have to get back,' she called from the centre, her voice strangely tight.

I thought she was annoyed at waiting so long for me to get in. For a moment we faced each other, white necks bared to the syrupy water. She looked at me, frowning.

'Your scalp is starting to burn. I should have made you bring your hat. Come on, we need to go.'

With a few deft strokes she was at the edge, thin cords of water winding around her legs as she pulled herself out. She was packing up the picnic basket, the enamel mugs clanging on her hooked fingers like dissonant bells.

'Could we come again another day?' I asked. I was confused, trying to interpret her haste. It was so hard with adults, especially the old ones. So tiring.

Her face emerged from inside her heavy cotton shirt, dark patches already blooming on her chest. Her lips ran straight across in a line. 'We'll see,' she said. 'I don't know.'

'Did you think there might be snakes in the water, Grandma? Is that why we had to get out?'

She turned her head towards me. She was suddenly very tall, like a horse rearing.

'You know, Geraldine' – her voice was high, I could hear the trace of Scots – 'I get a bit sick of all your silly little fears, at times. They really can seem quite, well, quite childish.'

Childish. It flashed out, bit into me, piercing, like a whip. Like a snake. She had never spoken to me like this. We had proper chats. She'd asked me what I thought of her new dress, whether I liked the colour, which was green. My favourite.

I watched the cows through the trees. They looked back at me, staring and chewing.

She gathered the last of the things, rearranged the brim of her dripping hat and stood waiting. We walked back to the house in silence, the basket knocking between us, my eyes full and stinging. I kept my head down, but the ground blurred up at me.

'We might go into town tomorrow,' she said at last. The dog was barking on the verandah. 'Would you like that?'

I was old enough to know that this was an apology, offered once, wrapped in thin paper. 'Yes,' I said. 'Town would be nice. I'd like that.' My voice sounded very small. Childish.

'We'll go tomorrow, then,' she said to me, softly.

She was my grandmother once more. But she kept looking ahead, her jaw clamped, her sensible black shoes crunching hard on the grass.

We never swam there again. By the next school holidays, she was a widow. On a bright morning in a snap-cold winter, men in dustcoats carried furniture and farm equipment into the yard. The sideboard teetered down the stairs, its mysterious drawers emptied and removed, its gap-toothed, brown face looking huge and defeated. An auctioneer in a greasy hat hammered his way through forty years until only the dry land, with its rough fences and its thirsty trees, remained. By the next day, two men in clean boots would be patting each other's suede shoulders, each levelling a proprietorial eye along the distant line of gums.

Strange how quickly a life can be shut down, closed like a door, or a book. She bought a small house on the edge of town in a bewildered flurry of loss. The old milk jug, looking suddenly shabby, filled the redundant space for a microwave. The bathroom was papered in black and white, an etching of a bare-breasted Spanish woman, repeating herself, buxomly, up the walls. Motes of sticky red earth walked into every corner, blazoned themselves across a once-hopeful cream carpet. With her cows gone, and the dry brown hill that had risen beyond the verandah lost, now, to strangers, her world shrank to church and pot plants, and muffled disapproval of the street's single mother.

She had every tree on the block cut down, still afraid of the bushfire that had once roared across the farm and loomed like an ogre at the foot of the back stairs.

Her new house contracted against us all. There could no longer be whole families together, no flat-voiced children giving concerts, no late-night card games for the adults, the generator humming into the empty night, laughter trailing into rooms like a friendly ghost.

I visited again, travelling alone on the bus, just as I had on that first unaccompanied trip. Now a cane field stretched into the horizon. Behind a half-shrugging hill, a highway pulsed. In the muggy air, my grandmother's house drooped beside its somnolent neighbours. We walked the town's main street, sheltered by the cool deep of the shops' overhead verandahs.

'Whose child is this?' they'd ask my grandmother in every store, sliding a mint across the age-smoothed counters, or poking in their cash registers for a spare coin to pass to me.

'This is one of Cynthia's,' my grandmother would say.

'Geraldine,' I'd tell them, scooping up the sweets and the money.

At night, we watched television. We lifted our heads to survey any car that passed by. The frayed bitumen crackled under the slow-turning wheels, each car moving warily, as if it hadn't meant to come this way at all.

The good dog, which by day kept to the lino, waited until the lights were out before taking up his usual position, stretched the full length of the sofa, like a tired man.

'Do you remember swimming in the "200" paddock?' she said to me. The question was so clear and unexpected that my hand jumped from the table in fright, as if a glass had spilled. 'I never liked swimming there,' she said.

I thought of the half-solid water, the prod of cold through my swimsuit, the membrane clay moving underfoot. I told her I felt the same.

'I was afraid of snakes,' I said. 'I thought there might be a snake in the water.' A barb of memory curved towards me like a tiny scythe. *Childish*. I was afraid of that, too.

She didn't seem to hear me.

'I always felt strange being there,' she said, quietly. 'But when you children were small it was nice for you to swim. And then the grandchildren, too, of course. They had so much in the city. That dam was all I could offer. I couldn't take them to the better waterholes; they were too far into the bush. Too dangerous on my own with little ones.'

I was going to correct her. Remind her, once again. She'd been confusing my name with my mother's for some time now. Quite regularly, she really seemed to believe that I was Cynthia. But she had not spoken of the farm for over a year, as if she'd forgotten it completely. So I didn't offer my usual prompt of 'I'm Geraldine, Grandma.' Instead, feeling a vague sense of unease, I moved to the upholstered chair facing hers, and waited.

'He poisoned them, you know,' she said.

I did not dare make a sound. Did not dare slide a word in against the pinprick of light. She wasn't looking at me, just speaking into the room, into the hot stillness.

'Reg Courtney. Across at Witney Station. Oh, you never liked him, Cynthia. Even as a toddler you were afraid of him. You used to run under my skirt, eyes bulging, and say, "The big man is here."'

I imagined my mother as a young child, watching their neighbour crossing the paddock on his enormous brown horse. She'd told me about him herself. A cruel man, she'd said. Treated his animals badly. Left the cattle too long without water.

My grandmother was staring at the wall, speaking as if she were reading words projected there on the flat beige.

'There was a group of Aborigines on the land,' she said. 'About six, I think. We'd seen them quite a few times over the years. Oh, I got an awful fright the first time – over near Sampson's Gully – saw them moving through the trees. I didn't expect to see anyone at all in those parts. They didn't bother us, though. Your father always felt it was best to leave them alone, let them get on with things in their own way. But he was unusual. There was a lot of hatred … dreadful. And when animals went missing or anything at all went wrong, well, it was easier to blame them. The farmers enjoyed it, I think. It banded them together ... stopped them fighting each other.'

She didn't turn her head. She watched the wall as if clues were forming there, letter by letter.

'Reg Courtney came across late one afternoon,' she said. 'He didn't get off his horse, just pulled up near us. Your father and I were near the front steps. We'd just got home from town. You'd run upstairs, Cynthia, as soon as you saw his horse coming. When he arrived, Reg was chuckling to himself ... I wondered whether he'd been drinking. He told us that some of the Aborigines had come around to his place. I won't repeat what he called them. Said they'd been hanging about near the holding yards – they'd taken to making damper and they wanted some flour. We just stood there, looking up at him. Wondering why he'd come. Wishing he'd go.'

My grandmother shifted in her seat. 'He had a dirty, rolled cigarette burning in one hand. The flame was almost touching his skin. Everything was so still; all we could hear was the horse breathing and that awful man sniggering. I couldn't take my eyes off the cigarette. Would he feel it, I wondered, when it touched his skin? Or would it burn straight through?'

She hunched her shoulders forward as if the air had suddenly cooled. 'At last he told us what he was talking about. "I gave them some flour, alright," he said, and he leaned right out of the saddle towards us. The leather creaked loudly, made a sound like a small animal. The long stalk of ash from his cigarette fell into the dust without losing its shape. I remember looking at the little tube of grey lying at your father's feet.'

My grandmother let out a deep breath. '"Arsenic flour." That's what he said. Almost in a whisper. Slow, like he enjoyed saying it. Then he threw down the last of the cigarette, turned his horse without another word, and galloped away. Your father was so upset, Cynthia.'

Outside our window, a young girl on a rusty bike leaned against the mailbox and stared in at us with a pink, defiant face.

'We tried to find them,' my grandmother went on, turning her head towards the street, not noticing the girl. 'Without saying a word about it, your father rode out early the next morning. He thought he might be able to get to them in time. Save them. He found nothing.'

My grandmother looked straight at me and frowned hard, momentarily surprised and irritated to discover that I was not her daughter. Her lips pressed in confusion. She smoothed the bodice of her dress with her hands, traced her bottom lip with a tentative finger as if checking that it was still there. She drew in a short, loud breath, like a single sob.

'We never saw them again. We wanted to tell the police but we were afraid of the Courtneys. Ever since that row over the new fences. You know we found one of our yearlings afterwards, mutilated, lying dead near our front gate. They could have made life very hard for us.'

Even I knew about the Courtneys and their grudges. Old Reg was still alive, walking with two sticks and an unbowed grimace. Except for an exiled son, never mentioned again, the extended clan still lived at Witney Station, farming and fighting.

The wooden clock from the dining room, perched now on a narrow shelf like the carapace of a rare turtle, sounded the hour, booming against the thin walls. Not registering this, my grandmother resumed watching the flat space in front of her, as if its blankness gave her clarity, or comfort.

'Once, at a sale yard,' she went on, her voice steady, 'Reg Courtney leaned across the fence and told your father that he'd left him a present on the land. At first we thought he meant that poor beast. Your father didn't answer; wouldn't speak a word to him.

'"Nice and close," Reg said. "Just to keep things friendly. Like neighbours." He touched his hat then, and walked away.

'Your father didn't tell me for a long time. Only when he was sick himself. He wanted to say it before he died. He'd looked for the bones, I know he did. I looked for them, too. There were a few times, before he was really ill, when we were out checking the bores. We'd catch each other's eye as we picked through the bush. We were always searching for them. But we'd never found anything. Could never prove anything. They were just gone.'

She sat for a long time. I didn't think she would say any more but, with a lift of her chin, she went on.

'One day, oh, many years later, not long before your poor father died, I was swimming at the "200". The water was quite shallow after that very hot summer. I don't think the level had ever been so low. I was out near the middle ... waiting for one of you. Goodness, that water was so cold. For the first time that I could ever remember, my feet could touch the bottom at the centre. I was pushing off from the clay, which was always very soft and muddy. That's what made the water so dark. I thought I felt something underfoot. Smooth and round. Bone. Not an animal – I'd know the crown of an animal. Then I knew what it was. At last I knew. The flash of it. It was like lightning striking the water. I suddenly remembered what Reg Courtney had said, all those years before. "Nice and close. Like neighbours." I was sure then, where they were.'

Her voice was rising, words beginning to tumble.

'I couldn't get out fast enough but I had to get the children out. No – it was just one. One child. It was one of yours, Cynthia. It was, I think, it was ... it was the oldest one.'

Her voice was curling into itself, following memory into its coiled depths. The name, my name, the memory of that day, was falling away. Sinking.

'I was swimming back. It was unbearable. I felt as if I were being pulled under. I had to get out. I was telling the children to get out. Who was it? Oh, it was Michael. Yes. Just the one child. Yes, I think it was Michael with me.'

There was no Michael, save for an infant brother of her own, who'd died of diphtheria just after she was born. The door was closing.

'What did you do, Grandma? After you felt the bones in the water?'

She turned to look at me, her head tilted in confusion. Her eyes scanned the room and drifted across the mean apron of concrete just beyond the front windows. At the edge of the road, the red dirt was crayon bright after the rain.

'Just look at that soil,' she said. 'It's uncanny, that colour. Oh, I know it's good for the crops but … well, I don't think I'll ever get used to it.'

She crossed her arms. Sat back in the chair as if overcome with fatigue.

'The water, Grandma?'

'Water? What water?' She looked straight at me for a long time, her eyes feeling their way around my face. She smiled. She was still quite beautiful, the proud way her head turned.

'Oh, Geraldine. I haven't made you any tea. You must have been waiting for ages. Did I nod off? Was it tea you wanted? Is that what you said?'

She was rising. Still strong-backed. Still a trace of the champion swimmer she had been. She lifted her big body from the chair. Just for a moment, she moved slightly to the left and right, as if not entirely sure where the kitchen lay. Then, with a small judder of recognition, she walked towards the back of the house with her rolling step.

'You just stay there and I'll do it,' she called. She was calm now, her mind washed clear. In a lot of ways, she seemed happy. 'You've been looking after me your whole visit, dear. Just relax. I'm sure I have coffee here somewhere.'

Cupboard doors were opening and shutting, opening and shutting.

'Let me see. Yes, here's some tea,' she called. 'You were talking about swimming. I was a very good swimmer at school. There's a big silver cup on the sideboard. Do you see it? That's mine. I'll be with you in a moment, Geraldine. And don't worry about that dog. He's a good fellow. He never comes onto the carpet.'

All the Perfumes

Rachel runs the stopper across her wrist, feels the smooth glass on her skin, the wet slide of it. There's a thrill of violets, a peppery trace of rose. An English scent. She imagines milky skies, soft rain, deep emerald hedgerows. She'd like to go there one day, she decides. One day. She watches the swipe of fragrance as it dries on her arm, waits for the embrace of flowers and spice. She never tires of this one. It makes her feel safe.

She looks out the window. A hazy Sydney evening, the bony husk of the Opera House still visible, far in the distance. Across the street, sheer-faced office buildings show no sign of life. The city is going home – silently, from this height. Lines of cars nose out of basements, push forward, disappear. Only the sound of the lifts exhaling in the shaft across the hall slips under her door. Tomorrow, she thinks, she might go outside.

It's suddenly dark but she doesn't bother with the lamp. She leans back in her chair, eyes closed. The fragrance wafts around her, delicate, intense. Rain. For some reason, today, this one reminds her of rain. Not here. At the farm, long ago, where it was precious.

When rain fell there, it was beautiful. Rachel would sit on the front steps and wait for the greenish tang of it to swirl towards her, drop its dusty posy of scent at her feet. Eucalyptus. Lemon myrtle. A hint of peppermint. Thin streamers of mist would catch, for a moment, in the top of the ghost gums, birds going crazy under the dripping leaves. Rain at last. But not enough. Never enough.

Rachel tries not to think of all the other days there. The way the ground set, stone-hard, underfoot. How everything drooped and faded, bleached to the horizon. Sometimes, in the distance, a dark cloud would scud by. She remembers standing on the verandah with her parents, silent as hunters, watching it track above the landscape. When the cloud disappeared from view, her father picked up his hat and left without a word.

Her mother grew roses. She planted them at the front of the house – a small, defiant circle of tended grass. Three preposterous bushes, struggling against oven-hot bricks. Rachel pictures her, carrying a basin from the kitchen. The silver arc of the water, flying. And the way it fell, solid as a hank of thick rope, the crack of it as it hit the ground. And the last of the cattle in the top paddock, staring.

Rachel shifts in her chair. She knows she shouldn't let herself doze. That she must not think about the farm.

But the hugging beauty of the scent carries her back there. Behind her flickering eyelids, she sees the grey-brown hills.

It was another dry storm. Late afternoon. Rachel was glad her father had gone to town. He would see the bank again, he'd told them. Stay with his brother while he was there. Back Wednesday.

There'd been lightning and a mauling wind, but only one brief shower, scurrying past. Everything was hot, pulsing out its aroma like a shout. Dust. Dead grass. The mineral bones of the land.

And there she is. Rachel running, her hair bobbing high, snatching leaves from the lemon myrtle, each one sheeny with a touch of damp. She'd check the dam, she told her mother. See if any of the rain had held. Her mother had looked back at her with a thin smile.

The dry grass whips Rachel's legs as she races down the long paddock. There's the spindly tangle of scrub, gravel as her shoes slide, the dam's crusty tiles of earth snapping under her feet.

And a hat – out of place – her father's hat, cartwheeled away, its empty crown tilted to the sky. She calls out for him, just once, before she lifts her head. She sees the red roof of the ute, tucked under the straggle of shrubs. And then, something hunched on the stones, a lifeless shape pooled in the last of the water, an arm flung wide. A blue-checked shirt she'd nuzzled a thousand times.

And the smell. The way it swarmed after her as she

shrieked and stumbled, her mother on the verandah, on the stairs, racing towards her, her skirt flaring against that hopeless patch of green. How night fell, at last, on a sobbing house, the lemon myrtle leaves still crushed in the curve of her fist, their foggy citrus consoling her, leading her into sleep.

A door slams down the hall. Rachel's startled awake, gulping air. She drops the stopper back into the bottle. It fits into place with a leaden clink. By tomorrow, she sees, it will be empty. She checks the others on the table, feels a wash of panic. All of the bottles have less than a quarter left. She trails her fingers across their tops like a caress, counting them. Twenty bottles. Only twenty left. Not enough, she thinks. Never enough.

And on the stairs, she'd swear it, that smell, rising.

Portal

Martin pushed the key into the lock but did not turn it. He did this every night when he got home. It was cold this evening, perhaps the first day he'd really felt it. Winter wasn't far away. The street was unusually quiet; everyone had gone in.

He put his bag down on the small square of concrete that served as a porch, pressed his forehead against the front door. Not for the first time, he marvelled at how solid the wood felt. Oak, he'd decided, long ago. He felt certain that the door had ended up here by accident, attached to his house in some sort of renovation mix-up. Perhaps it was meant for one of those big places on the terrace, near the park. It was not meant for this street, this house.

Right from the day they'd moved in, Martin had thought the rest of his place looked a little flimsy. Insubstantial. If a hurricane came barrelling through – an unlikely prospect in Luton, he had to admit – he imagined that the whole house would break apart in flat chunks, the wind scooping up the pieces, sending them eddying skywards, down to the roundabout and away. Perhaps those shards of his life would head south, towards London. Martin imagined the wallpaper that Shelley insisted on pasting over every damn flat surface skimming over trucks and cars and endless rooftops. He pictured the bedroom paper with its weird tangle of silver and lilac knots flashing overhead, people looking up in awe at the flying walls and the atrocious taste. But the door, this door, would remain, standing firm in all its panelled, woody glory. Standing like a portal to another life.

He thought about the young woman at the drycleaners that morning.

'Last name?' she'd said, without looking up.

She knew that the splashy stains on the bottom of his trouser legs were vomit. The work Christmas party, held on a damp evening in early October because 'we're flat out all December, aren't we team!' Martin grimaced at the memory of everyone sitting at that long table at the back of the local pub, wearing the cheap nylon Christmas hats that someone in Accounts had saved from last year.

Other drinkers had pointed and smiled indulgently.

'Like to get in early, you lot, don't you!' one old idiot had called as he passed, his bellowing laugh making everyone turn.

Martin had barely eaten a thing that night because, yet again, nobody had bothered to pre-order anything gluten-free. And that smartarse Dan saying, 'Come on, Marts, you've been sitting on that glass long enough. Here we go, mate. This'll do you good.'

The girl at the drycleaners had made pincers of her fingers and dropped his trousers into a red plastic bin. She had a tattoo on the inside of her finger. It read 'Love' in oddly old-fashioned script. It must have hurt, Martin thought.

'Birch,' he said to her.

'Is that with a "t"?' she asked, still not looking up, her love finger tapping on the keyboard.

'No. It's like the tree. Birch.'

She looked up at him then, her face expressionless.

'You're far too young,' Martin said, 'to have heard of being birched at school.'

His own father had been caned with birch twigs when he was a boy. 'Never did me a bit of harm, son,' he'd always insisted, though not long before he died he'd broken down and sobbed when a man smacked his kid in the Aldi car park.

The love-finger girl, who was no more than eighteen, gave a small nod. It was hard to tell whether she was agreeing that, yes, she was far too young for whatever he was going on about, or deciding that this loser and possible pervert, who couldn't hold his drink, was never going to just spell out his friggin' name and let her get on with it.

'Wednesday,' she said, and slid a green ticket across the counter. When Martin reached out to take it, her hand flew up as if the ticket had been electrified.

It was beginning to feel really cold on the doorstep. Martin picked up his bag. The yappy little mutt at the corner had started up again. In the house beside him, the new people had all the lights on, as if they wanted to celebrate every inch, every beam and cornice of their new lives. In the narrow garden bed that separated the two houses, a smirking plaster gnome grinned in the spilling light.

Behind his own front door, Martin could hear his young daughter wailing, 'But I want it!'

Shelley was shouting, too. 'I'll give you what you deserve in a minute, my lady.'

Martin took a deep breath. He turned the key, pushed the door. The preposterous, heavy oak door on his weak-jointed house.

It opened without a sound.

The Way It Sounds

Uncle Hector was the best because he had a hole in his neck.

'Can we see your bullet wound?' we'd ask.

'My wooooound?' he'd say, dragging out the sound like a ghost. But he always smiled when he said it, so we knew it was funny. He was a good joker, Uncle Hector.

Then he'd say, 'Attention!' like we were in the army and he was the boss. We'd line up, taking it in turns to put our finger along the little trench at the back of his head.

'That was lucky, Uncle Hector,' someone would say, and he'd ruffle our hair. 'You're telling me. Lady Luck was on double duty that day, eh?'

Once, one of the cousins said, 'Uncle Hector, what happened to the bullet? Where did it go after your neck?'

And he didn't smile then. Or make a joke. He just rubbed his hands together like he was really cold. They made a scratching sound.

'Straight into the head of my mate,' he said, and his face went red, even redder than at Christmas.

'Does he have a wound, too?' someone asked.

And he smiled, but only his mouth looked happy. He patted our shoulders and told us to skedaddle.

Later, we saw him in the garden, way up near the back fence. He was digging fast, then wiping his face on his sleeve. It wasn't very hot that day.

I asked my mother what Uncle Hector was doing.

'Just digging,' she said. 'He'll be in soon.'

I watched him from the upstairs window. He was very old but still strong. The shovel made an ugly sound going in. The sound of metal, hitting hard.

The Painting

'It's worth a pile,' she said, her breaths coming harder today, 'or so your father reckoned.'

In the silence that settled between them, he watched her insect fingers curl and uncurl around one corner of the frame.

'You don't deserve it,' she said, 'but there's no one else to give it to.'

She pushed the painting across the counterpane that had been on her bed since before his father left. Watching the picture scrape across the cloth, he saw how filthy the bed linen was – the unwashed colours still jauntily bright, the nodding daisies mired in a field of grime.

Beneath the cover lay her rasping form, her yellow hair fanned out, her eyes filtering the last of the light through aqua-tinted lids as fragile as ancient lace. With night coming on, she stirred a little. Deep within her frail bones, something was rattling to the surface. She stared hard at the ceiling, seeing beyond the swags of web, the tongues of paint arching down.

'Rory deserved it,' she said.

There were no more words, just sounds. Weak and girlish in the end. A breeze rose and pushed through the drapes like a visitation. Soon after that, he had no mother. He had an oil painting framed in heavy black, the wood as thick as a child's arm.

As he watched the still form, the night cooling around his shoulders, it didn't seem like a bad exchange.

Frank said he had no call for paintings, but Eddie saw him lick his lips. That nervous flash of tongue. He'd seen it before, many times. Frank always did it when an easy profit drifted into his pawnshop like the scent of blood.

'I don't know, Eddie ... might take it for my own place,' he said. 'The missus might like it. She likes a good view, so she does.'

But Frank had rested his fingertips on the frame for a second too long. Eddie had noticed. If they touch it, they want it. That's what the old fella used to say. And he knew a thing or two about selling. And touching.

He watched Frank lean towards the canvas, peer at its leaden sky, the way the cloud thinned in one corner, the oils there as light as watercolours, a mere tincture of lavender and coral. With surprising delicacy, Frank traced a finger over the small symbols, mostly circular, that were carved into all sides of the frame.

'How old is this thing?' Frank said.

Frank wanted to know where he got it, Eddie knew.

But he would not ask. It was the one question Frank would never ask.

Eddie shrugged. 'No idea.'

Frank leaned closer to the painting. He was smelling it. Eddie had seen him do that before, long ago when he was barely tall enough to see over the countertop. 'You can tell a lot by sniffing something, boy,' he'd told Eddie then. With a jolt of shame, Eddie remembered his father, leaning on the counter beside him, tittering like a fool.

But Frank wasn't telling him anything this time. He knew the game as well as Eddie did: make an offer, then do not speak. The one who speaks first loses.

Eddie squinted out the front window into the afternoon traffic. Frank followed his gaze. They chewed on their secrets in silence, watching the cars pass. It was quiet behind the reinforced glass.

'Frank, I think I'll keep it after all,' Eddie said, surprising himself. He took a side of the frame in both hands, felt the strange ridges in the wood. 'It's sort of growing on me.'

Frank let his weight slacken back onto his cushioned stool, one thick forearm still resting on the glass counter. Under a pelt of ginger hair lay a faded tattoo: an anchor. Eddie stared, marvelling that he'd never noticed it before. As far as Eddie knew, Frank had spent the last forty years in this dingy shop. Bar the ferry, he doubted Frank had ever been on a boat in his life.

'Did you grow up in Brooklyn?' Eddie said.

'What?'

'Where did you grow up?' Eddie had no idea why he needed to know.

Frank snorted. 'Mind your own business.' He cleaned some dust off the counter with the flat of his hand. 'You wouldn't believe me even if I told you.'

'True enough.'

Rewrapping the painting in an old sheet, Eddie could feel Frank's eyes on him, taking in his new shirt, the cleaner hair.

Frank nodded at the painting. 'Getting a bit cultured in your old age, are you, Eddie?'

They half-smiled at each other with something close to affection.

'I'll see you again,' Eddie said. He picked up the painting, tapped a pink box on the counter with his free hand. It was empty. 'And stay off those doughnuts, Frank. They'll kill you in the end.'

'S'pose it's croissants and macchiatos for you these days, is it, Eddie?'

Eddie smiled, but didn't turn back. The traffic noise pushed through the opened door. Outside, the air was still warm but autumn hung in the wings, pursing its lips. Eddie felt his skin prickle; the frame held solid under his arm.

Dear old Mother was right, he thought. This painting's worth something.

Oblivious to the blaring horns, he crossed against the swooping traffic and headed uptown.

★

Walter Fennell had his name on a brass plate by the door, like a doctor. High marble steps led up to a narrow, white-tiled entrance. A miniature tree filled one corner, its leaves trimmed into a perfect cone, the tip sharp enough to scratch a hand like an unfriendly pet. Walter, wary of topiary thieves, would wheel his potted tree in and out each day on its small castors. He kept the place immaculate. More than once, Eddie had seen Walter on his knees with a dustpan and brush, scooping up breakaway leaves and rogue pieces of litter that had funnelled up from the street.

The door would be locked, Eddie knew. He'd been here once before. There was a bell to press. Inside, Walter would be watching the entry from a judicious angle, his finger hovering over a white button on his desk. If he chose, the glass door would swing back as if held by an invisible footman.

Eddie knew that Walter had not always had the face of a disappointed man. There'd been a big write-up in the paper, years back, after the opening night. For some reason his mother had cut the piece out and kept it. He'd found the clipping just after she died. There was Walter, looking haughty and intense in a spectacularly good suit. He was so sure of himself then, the way he tilted his chin to the camera. Sure that earnest knots of people in black clothes would continue to gather before his door. That they would glide around his white box of a gallery, listening to him enthusing about power and authority, marvelling at the painted squares hung in careful light. Buyers will come,

Walter's confident face had said. Come to press the flesh of his emerging artists, standing, nervous as fawns, on the edge of a wineglassed crowd.

But they did not come. The gallery sat, now, like the egg of a rare bird in a nest of plain shops, a tattoo parlour two doors down.

Back in those early years, Walter would never have looked at someone like me, Eddie thought, inspecting his reflection in the glass door. But now, Eddie sensed another slow week in the art world, and knew to wait for the buzz. He thought of his mother, snipping out Walter's story, and wondered.

There was the smallest click. Eddie knew Walter could see the painting, and that he would not be able to resist. The door pulled back.

He hoped Walter wouldn't remember his last visit.

'Mr Reynolds, isn't it?' Walter said.

Eddie saw that Walter was going to remain at his desk so that he'd have to approach him like a naughty schoolboy. Asshole, Eddie thought. Walter looked a bit thinner, a bit pinker, but when he stood up he was still ramrod straight in his glossy black shoes.

'No medals, today, I trust,' Walter said, a wraith of a smile under his moustache.

Eddie felt heat in his cheeks, but kept his voice chipper. 'Not today, no.'

The last meeting, two years before, had not gone well. Eddie had been trying to off-load his Uncle Ivan's war medal, back at the height of things. Or the depth of things. With not much more than flared nostrils and a bit of adept sniffing, Walter had made it abundantly clear exactly what he thought of a man trying to hock his family's one shred of military pride for drink money. Eddie was back outside with the pointy tree before he could say Dardanelles.

In the end, Frank had come to the party on the medal. Despite all the pawned tat in his shop, he had a market somewhere for good war stuff. He'd got Eddie a great price; at least he'd thought it was. Might've been worth ten times the money. All gone now, of course. The medal was the last of it. The drinking, the snorting, everything. But some of Uncle Ivan's military discipline must have rubbed off, Eddie thought. The way I pulled up before the last jump. Before the cliff.

Walter broke into his thoughts. 'You have something you wish to show me, Mr Reynolds?'

Eddie laid the painting on the table and began to pull back the cloth, Walter wincing at the prospect of table scratches. When he saw the painting, he was silent for a full minute.

'Where did you get this?' Walter said.

'I inherited it,' Eddie told him.

'I see,' Walter said, scanning the room as if amazed to find himself in an art gallery.

Eddie, hating his own need to explain further, said, 'It was my mother's. She's dead now.'

'I see,' Walter said again.

There was another full minute of silence, Walter staring down at the painting. Eddie watched him run his hand along one side of the frame, his fingers hovering about the wood as if reading its aura.

'I'm sorry, Mr Reynolds,' Walter said, 'but I simply cannot help you. It's not my field. You'll need a specialist.'

'A specialist?' Eddie was genuinely surprised. 'Can you recommend anyone?'

Walter wrinkled his forehead as if the question had caused his gut to spasm. 'Recommend? I don't think so.' He waved around the room with an airy, imprecise hand. 'You see where my expertise lies – I deal almost exclusively in modern art.' He hesitated. 'Not medals. Not ... paintings like this one.'

Eddie saw that Walter had a small shake in his head. He wondered whether it was Parkinson's or merely revulsion.

'You must know someone who understands these things,' Eddie pressed. He could see Walter swallowing his irritation.

Walter leaned across the desk and wrote a name and address on a piece of paper. 'You could try this place,' he said. 'They may be able to help you in some way.'

Eddie noted the languid 'may' but took the details. He saw that Walter also had a bad shake in his hand. Maybe the uptight old bastard is on the dry, too, Eddie thought.

'You have to be aware, Mr Reynolds,' Walter said, 'that there will be significant costs involved in obtaining precise information on your ... acquisition.' He took a pressing interest in the pile of catalogues fanned in a perfect wheel on the corner of his desk, neatened one errant spine. 'I really think that's all I can tell you,' he said.

Eddie exhaled hard. 'Oh, I see,' he said. 'My mistake. I thought you'd have a sort of broad knowledge about art. You know, a kind of general knowledge about your field. Like, for instance, I know a fair bit about gardening, even though my real speciality is lichen, if you can believe that.'

Walter looked like he did not, although it was perfectly true.

'I guess it's different in the art world,' Eddie went on, sauntering across the blond wood floor towards a chair, as if he meant to sit and chat about life's daily setbacks. 'Never mind, I guess I'll see what this' − he waved the piece of notepaper towards Walter − 'specialist can tell me.'

Eddie turned away from the chair at the last moment, Walter already beginning to gape at the thought of him actually taking a seat. Eddie allowed himself a small smile. His father would have been proud. He felt tempted to whistle.

And it had worked. Walter Fennell was niggled. He didn't get that brass plate for nothing, Eddie thought.

'It's British,' Walter said. 'A London street scene. I'm sure of it. Central London, almost certainly. Probably looking east.' He ran his eyes around the frame. 'The wood is carved in a curious way. The markings are not typically English. The painting could be two hundred years old, perhaps more.'

Walter wiped a non-existent speck of dust from the desk with one finger. 'I strongly recommend that you have it assessed and insured,' he told Eddie. 'And you might consider restoration. It has not been properly cared for.'

Walter pressed the button with a small look of triumph.

He loves that freakin' button, Eddie thought.

The front door opened with a buzz.

'But is it valuable?' Eddie said, just to annoy him.

Walter's high colour was feverish now. He stood up. 'Of course it is, if it's genuine. Now, if you'll excuse me, I have an appointment.' He zipped his leather valise, and nudged Eddie towards the door without touching him.

But as Eddie had rewrapped the painting, he'd seen Walter's eyes rest on it a moment too long. It's genuine, he was sure. Walter didn't want to buy the painting, he wanted to save it from someone like him.

Eddie stopped at the door, pointing at the tree with the wrapped edge of the painting. 'I thought you'd like to know that you're overwatering your ficus. They don't tend to like it.'

The door hissed closed behind him.

1827. Shadwell, East London.

At first, Thomas Reynolds didn't think the man was still alive. He felt afraid, desperately afraid, but there was no one else to help him. Fox Lane was deserted. He went to the edge, his feet slipping, leaned out across the oily black water, pulled the man ashore by the sleeve with all his strength. Just breathing.

And who is he? Such a heavy coat. Very nearly the death of him. Thomas touched the fine stitching near the collar. It was good once, but worn now, almost to a thread. With one arm, he dragged the man home on the great flail of his coat, its seams tearing as he went. *A dog stared from the corner. No other soul.*

'Get a blanket, Susannah. And a pillow. Hurry.'

Thomas tried not to think about the water. *The way it had reached up to him when he stepped in, the freezing wrap of it on his flesh. The bad dreams would return, he knew.*

'I know it's late, Susannah.' Thomas' voice was loud over her protests at the front door. *He turned the man on his side, heard a single gurgle. He could have got his throat cut, Thomas thought, wandering around near there. A stranger.*

'I don't know what he was doing by the pond, Susannah. Maybe he was hungry or something.' *Thomas looked down at the sharp cheekbones. He looks thin, true enough.*

Susannah was waking up the whole building with her carping.

'I know there's nothing but reeds in that pond,' Thomas called back. *As if he could forget. He would never forget.*

'Yes, Susannah,' Thomas agreed, trying to keep the tremble out of his voice, 'they're shocking, those reeds, the way they pull you down. They very nearly took this one.'

He's not English, by the looks of him, Thomas thought. Not a sailor with those boots. 'I didn't put myself in any danger, Susannah,' he called down the passageway. 'I just pulled the man out with my good arm. And, no, I wasn't afraid in the least.'

Thomas lifted him as best he could, pulled him inside along the narrow hall, curled him onto a patch of bare floor. He stripped away

the drenched clothes. He saw the bony ribs, a rise and fall of the chest
so minute that he wondered whether he'd imagined it. He pressed the
blankets close around the man's still frame. No money in his pockets,
just an old sketchbook, ruined now. And a tiny paintbrush.

'Heavens, Susannah, I don't know where he's from. Does
it matter when the man's half-dead?' Odd little carvings on the
handle of the brush. 'I need some dry clothes for him. Bring me my
new shirt. I said bring it, Susannah.'

Thomas smoothed the dark hair back from the man's face.
A high forehead. A strong jaw. He hails from somewhere well east
of here, that's for sure. Thomas felt grateful for the good fire, still
burning so late. The brightness calmed him.

'Let's get him in nearer the heat, Susannah. Help me pull him
over. Come, woman, while there's still a chance.'

Eddie stripped everything. Burned the blue counterpane.
Pulled apart the bed that his mother had sobbed and died
in. Where there were carpets, he tore them away, the tacks
at the edges gripping the last of the weave like indignant
gremlins. In the hall, the threadbare carpet proved thinner
than an underlay of compacted dust that rose up like a
ghoul and billowed down the steps and into the street. He
hired a contraption – a kind of blowtorch – and made the
paint on the walls and ceilings pucker and blister before
slicing it away with a scouring blade. When everything was
purged, he set up home amidst the shaved surfaces, the last,
defeated shreds of colour herded into the highest corners
and ignored.

In the main room, Eddie hung his painting. A single square of colour on a stretch of bare wall. And he watched over it like a parent: proud, entranced, anxious.

Eddie had his mother's old tin box, garish in deep reds and golds, balanced in his lap. The ancient tiled gate, its shape bulging from the lid's flat surface, felt pleasing under his fingertips. Turkish delight. The impossible sweetness of it. The strange happy taste still in his mouth after so long.

There were mostly photos inside the box now, a few papers and clippings. Walter's smug face on the curling newsprint, an advertisement for ladies' dancing classes that pulled his throat tight with sadness, and a childish picture of a red car that made him want to weep out loud. *Love from Rory* was scrawled on the back in generous loops.

Strange, Eddie thought, how the golden child always lets the side down by dying young. That was Rory. Mother's pet, no doubt about it, but so bright and funny and good that you couldn't hate him if you tried. He even had the blond hair. And the good teeth. They always have good teeth, Eddie thought. Seeing Rory lying on the slab, one powder-rimmed hole in his chest, Eddie felt sure that he still didn't have a single hole in any of his teeth.

Rory had gone into the ground as perfect as he'd always been, Eddie thought. Except for the place where cousin Mikey had shot him with the hunting gun that his father had insisted he was old enough to have. In the excitement of being eligible to kill things, Mikey forgot about not pointing, about unloading, and all the other stuff that had whistled through his empty head.

He wiped out my brother with one clean shot, Eddie thought. Rory had gone down without a murmur, like the good boy he was. Just a small look of surprise on his beautiful face.

Then Mother was left with me, Eddie thought. The *other* son. I got the Reynolds nose but my father's irksome habits. And even worse, she was left with Dad. That hollow laugh of his. The heavy footsteps on the stairs, hours late. The empty pockets. After Rory, there was nothing. Just a furious, staring blankness, one to another.

'You're home,' his mother used to say as his father breasted the door.

'That's what it looks like,' he'd reply, throwing down his key on the table.

The clink of forks on plates. Little else.

Eddie wondered what things had been like at their best. And when that had been. There was no marriage certificate in the tin box. His mother had never given up her maiden name. He and Rory were Reynolds, just like her. She didn't care what people said. She was always edging away from him, Eddie thought. We were her future, Rory and me. Especially Rory.

But sometime after Rory died, his mother had stopped edging in any direction. Eddie couldn't put a time on it. All he knew was that when he was still half a boy, she had taken to her bed, rolled towards the wall, and mused for decades on golden chances lost.

Eddie wasn't lonely. He was done with people, as he'd lately told the guy at the bakery. With his family gone – beautiful Rory, his aching mother, the old man with his laughs and his rages – he'd got used to his life of seclusion. He was close enough to happy.

He didn't need much money. Just enough to get by. He put up a notice at the bakery, left a few more fluttering on lampposts and walls. To his surprise, there was a good response. He began to make reasonable cash, gardening for executives who lived nearby, too busy or disinclined to even water their pot plants. He liked the work. It was solitary and involved keeping things alive. Both suited him now.

There were some bad days. They still came, even without the drink. Eddie had not expected that. On these days, only vaguely aware of the traffic and the endless clang of the gate down to the basement, he would sit on the tapestry sofa that he'd dragged into the main room, staring at his painting. He would wonder about the times when it had hung on other walls, in other places. He pictured it shrouded in the backs of wardrobes, or interred in travelling chests, the great ocean juddering outside.

He called it *The London Painting*. There was no other name. No signature, no frame-maker's mark. He knew every inch of it. My inheritance, he thought. In his solitary life, that street scene was his crowd. It was all the people he needed.

Among them one day, he saw a boy.

There were about ten people in the picture, mostly ranged along a busy street. Wooden buildings pressed impossibly close on either side; slick laneways branched from the main thoroughfare and cornered into darkness. There were animals and carts, two men chatting, one wiping his brow. There was a face at one of the overhead windows, a laughing woman on the step, a travelling locksmith hanging bunches of keys as big as cabbage heads.

There were children, too. He'd thought he knew them all. The one leaning towards the fruit vendor, the two grubby ones kicking a ball under a cart. In the bottom corner, a round-shouldered boy was dragging his reluctant horse into the frame and onwards.

And now, another boy.

A boy Eddie had certainly not seen in the painting when he showed it to Frank, or to Walter. A boy leaning around the corner from the laneway, his blond hair curling out from under an enormous cap, a quizzical look on his face. The jacket he was wearing was too big for him, and it hung open at the neck. Beneath the dark wool, a patch of red bloomed like a poppy on his chest.

The face was unmistakable. It was Rory.

Eddie sprang to his feet. Damp, he thought. The plumbing in this old building complained half the day and most of the night. The ceilings still bore faint blooms of past disasters, tattooed into the fleshy plaster. It's damage from a leaking pipe, he thought. That was it. Eyes playing tricks.

Eddie ran his finger lightly across the figure of the boy. Bone dry. He looked around, half expecting some hideous prank. The apartment was as still as a museum.

He got out the tin box of photos and keepsakes, scrabbling among the papers until he found what he was looking for. It pained him to look at it. A photo of Rory taken at Mikey's party, just days before the end. Mikey and Rory, first cousins, arms draped around each other. Rory with his square white teeth, Mikey grinning into the camera with his bland and stupid face.

After Rory died, Eddie's mother had pulled out all the other photos of Mikey and her brother's family and shredded them into confetti with her pointed fingers. She had thrown the tiny scraps out the back window and watched them flit towards the East River on a stiff breeze. She had spared this one, the last of her magnificent dead boy. There he stood, entwined, inseparable, looped around his killer.

As Eddie held the photo up to the painting he was already telling himself that this solitary life was not doing him much good. *Those imagined fancies of yours.* That's what his mother used to call his childhood nightmares, her words meeting him in the hall, turning him back to his terrifying bed.

But, side by side, photo and painting, a stranger could have seen it in a moment. It was him.

Eddie went out immediately, leaving his jacket on its peg. He walked until well past nightfall, deaf to the rattle of the city, thinking of Rory, feeling truly afraid for the first time since those nightmares, since the flash of Mikey's gun with its towering noise reverberating around the barn, and Rory falling back and lying intolerably still. And the footsteps from the big house, and the shouts as they came, and the ending of things.

By the time Eddie got back to his apartment, it was almost light. He was cold but at least the night was dry. He'd accidentally left his front door open to the hall. The painting will be gone, he told himself, his feet on the stairs. That face will be gone.

No one had come in. No one had scooped up his few possessions. But when he walked into the main room he could see at a glance that no one had left. The tiny figure was still there. Rory, looking straight at him.

Eddie lasted just over a fortnight before heading back to Frank. Each morning he would check the painting, his heart gonging loud in his chest like the old clock in the study, long ago. And every time, rounding the corner, there was Rory, the quizzical look, the blaze of red on his chest. Was the red spreading? Surely it looked bigger?

By the time Eddie found himself rustling in the desk drawer for a ruler, fully intending to take the measurements of a blaze of red on a dead brother in a centuries-old painting, he knew he couldn't do this alone. Rory would have gone into the pawnshop with their dad on at least one occasion. Frank would know.

★

Frank looked hard at him, and didn't speak. They both listened to Frank's breathing, its occasional wet crackle. The clamour of the morning rush outside was dulled by the shop's thick glass. The place felt oddly safe.

Frank drummed his fingers on the counter, pointed to the figure halfway up the painting. 'You're asking me whether this looks like your brother? Your dead brother?'

Eddie told him again. The kid on the corner. The blond kid. He wasn't there before. It was Rory.

Again, the long, silent look. Frank leaned back on his stool. 'Jesus,' he said, at last, turning the corner of the painting away from his chest as if it were a pointed gun. 'You're getting more like your mother every day, Eddie. It's not normal what you're asking me.'

Eddie's temper flared without warning. Sleep had been scarce. 'I know it's not fucking normal,' he hissed through his teeth.

Frank raised an eye from the painting. A man outside the front window was cupping his face, peering in. Frank nodded towards the closed sign with a tiny derisive movement that sent the onlooker stepping back in surprise, off up the street at a pace.

Eddie was finding it hard to keep the whole mess in perspective. 'Just tell me,' he said. 'Did you ever meet Rory?'

'Yeah. He came in a good few times with your dad,' Frank said. 'Nice kid, he was. Quiet. Kept his hands to himself and didn't have to be told twice. Not a cheeky little brat like you.'

Eddie was not in the mood for Frank's banter. 'Does this kid look like him or not?' he said, feeling as if he could reach across the counter and pummel Frank's jowly pink face. He softened his tone. 'Just tell me what you think.'

Frank peered into the painting. 'From what I remember, yeah, it could be him alright. But, listen, Eddie ...'

Eddie slid the photograph from his pocket, held it up. 'Look, this is Rory.' He jabbed his finger at the smiling boy. 'My mother took this photo two days before he died. This is what he looked like at the end. Fifteen years old. Does this look like the kid in the painting or not?'

Frank looked at the photograph, then down to the painting. He had a good eye. He barely hesitated.

'It's him,' he said.

The ringing had been going on for a while. Eddie was dozing on the couch. He'd forgotten about the old phone in the spare room. His father had always insisted on calling that room the study, but there was never any study done there, not that he recalled. He remembered being thrown against the desk on more than one occasion. A kind of education.

Buried under a tipping pile of books and curling magazines, Eddie found the handset.

'How did you get this number?' Eddie said.

'And hello to you, Eddie,' Frank said. 'Same number it's always been. I used to ring your dad about ... stuff. Never mind. I was just ringing to see if you're okay, that's all. I didn't have any other contact number.'

Eddie said he was fine. It sounded too sharp when he was genuinely touched. There was a long pause. Down the line, he heard the bell ring in Frank's shop. 'I'm fine, Frank, really,' Eddie assured him. 'Listen, sorry about the whole painting thing.'

'Forget it,' Frank said. 'I'll get you again.'

Eddie smiled. 'I'm sure you'll do that.'

'You know me, Eddie. Hang on, I've got to get rid of this asshole.'

Eddie heard the bell on Frank's door sound again. He wondered how Frank made a living at all. Remembered Uncle Ivan's medal.

'Sorry,' Frank said. 'Now, Eddie, there's another reason why I'm ringing you. It's about the painting. I remembered something.'

'Go on,' Eddie said. The cord of the old phone reached into the hall. Rory was looking back at him through the doorway.

'Well,' Frank said, 'you know I liked your dad. You could have a good laugh with him. Yeah, I know he was a bit hard on you kids. Same thing as me, I guess: too much booze.'

He wasn't hard on both kids, Eddie thought, just me. But – the memory surprised him – Rory used to shrink back from their father sometimes, when he walked too close. 'Go on, Frank.'

'Came to me the other night,' Frank said. 'The missus

was going on about us being married forty years. As if I'd want to celebrate the worst goddamn mistake of my whole life.' He laughed at himself with a wheezy chortle. Eddie guessed he hadn't tried this on his rather fearsome wife. 'Anyway, my mind was wandering, and I suddenly remembered, clear as day – your dad told me about a weird painting that your mother had. It's got to be the same one.'

Eddie waited while Frank coughed down the line. 'It is,' Eddie said.

'Right,' Frank said. 'Well, you might know this already but I'll say it anyway, since I've rung up. Your dad told me it was handed down through your mum's family, but here's the thing: she hated it. She was so shit scared of it she kept it wrapped up in a box or something. She wanted to get rid of it but she couldn't for some reason.'

'What was she scared of?' Eddie said.

'Dunno. Look, Eddie, I wasn't taking a whole heap of notice of what your dad was on about, to be honest. I was starting to think he was getting a touch of your mother's way about him.'

Eddie felt a stab of loyalty. 'What do you mean "my mother's way"?'

'No offence, Eddie. But you know she was a bit … what my grandma used to call *fey*. You know, F. E. Y.' Frank was proud of his Scrabble skills. 'It means kind of connected with the supernatural.'

Eddie was watching the painting. 'I know what it means, Frank. Why did Dad tell you about the picture?'

Frank snorted. 'Wanted me to buy it, of course. What the hell else would he be doing other than trying to make a buck?'

'When was this?' Eddie said. He could hear Frank tapping his pencil on the shop counter.

'Oh, ages ago. I don't know. Years.' The tapping was like a drumbeat. A heartbeat. 'Oh, hang on,' Frank said, 'I do know. It was just before your brother was killed. I thought your dad was avoiding me but then I found out about Rory.'

Eddie was looking at the faces staring out of the frame.

'But, Eddie,' Frank went on. 'Here's the important bit. Bet you don't know this. You know the medal? You know, the war medal, the one I sold for you?'

'I remember,' Eddie said.

'Ivan. Name stuck in my head,' Frank said. 'Crazy Russian name for a kid in the British Army. Anyway, he was your mother's uncle, not yours. S'pose you know that. You couldn't have met him. Got killed in the First World War. Posthumous medal, of course. Barely more than a teenager, like half those poor bastards. Anyway, Eddie, here's the weird bit. Your mother reckoned she could see him in the painting. That's what your dad told me. That's what scared her. She reckoned he just appeared.'

The hairs on Eddie's neck prickled, like a creature catching the scent of an unseen predator. 'I'll call you back, Frank,' Eddie said. He put the receiver down on the floor.

There was a round-shouldered boy pulling a reluctant horse into the frame and onwards. His coat was streaked with grime, oddly blackened on one side. Eddie moved closer to the canvas. Beneath the gape of the coat he could see it: the boy was in uniform.

A dial, for Chrissake. Eddie's forefinger moved clockwise until he found the right number. He listened to the ratchet purr as the wheel returned. He had his mother's old address book balanced on his lap. He peered at her jagged writing on the ivory-coloured paper.

The phone rang on in Ohio. Eddie was about to put down the receiver.

'How yer doing?' The voice was happy. Expectant.

Eddie knew it was Mikey but he didn't speak.

'Hello? Who is this?' Mikey said into the silence, his voice steeling just a fraction. There was the sound of machinery in the background. A tractor, perhaps.

'It's me, Mikey. It's Eddie.'

'Eddie?' There was a long pause. 'Jesus. Cousin Eddie?' Mikey knew who it was; the only people who ever called him Mikey were his relatives. 'God, Eddie. I thought it was town, about the thresher, I've been waiting for ages, all morning ...' He rallied himself. 'So, hey, Eddie, good to hear from you. How are you?' Dread thickened his voice. 'Are you around here, or something?'

'I'm in Brooklyn,' Eddie said.

Mikey blew out a long, relieved breath. 'Right, right,' he said.

'You know Mum is dead,' Eddie said.

'Yeah, yeah, I heard. I was real sorry. Poor Aunt Anne. Hard for you.'

Not really, thought Eddie, remembering the near-empty chapel at the funeral parlour. A feeling close to hate pressed in at his temples. 'Listen, Mikey, I need to talk to you about something.'

'Right, okay,' Mikey said. He sounded punch-drunk.

'Listen, I …' The receiver felt heavy at Eddie's ear. 'Mikey, I need to talk to you about Rory.'

Mikey's reaction was instant, electric. 'Aw, shit. For God's sake, Eddie. I'm trying to run a farm here. I'm trying to get on with things. That whole business was … that was a long time ago. What happened that day, what happened to Rory, it was just terrible. I felt so bad, but you know … you could never get over it. Not any of us. But we were just …' Mikey's words cornered and turned back, defiant. 'No, I can't talk about it. Listen, I gotta go, Eddie. The thresher. I can't. You know, we were just, we were just …'

The line went dead. We were just kids, Eddie thought.

Eddie was trying to remember the last time he'd driven a car. Must be five years, at least. Miami? That stupid green Chrysler. That poor lost girl from Nebraska, the way the heat seemed to consume her whole, like a python. He was relieved those times were gone.

He pressed the accelerator of the rental car. The old road hadn't changed much. Maybe a bit smoother, in parts. Farmland stretched away in all directions. He felt his mood lift. It would do him good to be out of Brooklyn for a while.

He'd felt a pang that had scared him, leaving the painting. He'd thought about bringing it, but decided that was just too weird, even for a man who was waking three times a night like a father checking on his infant. Checking on Rory.

He'd worried about thieves. Nearly every apartment in his building had been turned over at least once although, strangely enough, never his place. There's nothing to steal anyway, he decided. Never was. And who'd want a dark old painting full of dead faces? Not me, thought Eddie, and the notion startled him. For the first time, he thought about his mother's last words. *Rory deserved it.* What the hell had Rory deserved?

Eddie found he remembered these last straight roads very well, even some of the houses. Soon, after the dog-leg corner, he would crest a long, smooth hill, and the farmhouse would be there, red-roofed against its picked-clean, yellow slopes. And the ghost of a barn, and the memory of the way its two huge doors had hung slightly aslant, its cavernous spaces darkly glimpsed, the hay stacked high. And the spirits of lost children, waiting.

Mikey had been a big teenager. 'You'll be the image of your father,' the aunts had clucked every Christmas. No one seemed to notice that Mikey's father was a thick-necked behemoth with hands like dirt-encrusted spades, and a forehead as broad as the unused table in the good dining room. But as Eddie pressed his eye to a crack in the wall, watching his cousin walking towards him, he was surprised to see that most of Mikey's growing had been over by the time he was killing Rory.

Eddie guessed that Mikey would not usually come out to the barn this late. But he would have seen the pale glow of the lantern in the pig-eyed windows, high up near the roof. Light, where there are no fixed electrics, could mean thieves, maybe even a fire. Mikey would come.

In the last strands of the evening sun, he could see Mikey getting closer, his face creased in agitation. He looks a whole lot better than me, Eddie thought. Across the crook of Mikey's arm lay a shotgun, its split barrel carefully pointing down at the foot-stamped earth. Eddie took a seat on a hay bale. He watched the lantern in its round pool of light, and waited.

Mikey pulled on one of the doors and it opened without a sound. Eddie felt the breeze almost at once. He knew that Mikey could not see him from the doorway. He heard him crack the shotgun home. A pair of pigeons cooed a warning to each other. A strange buzz played in Eddie's head.

'Who's there?' Mikey sounded afraid. Eddie wondered how often, here alone, Mikey had jumped at shadows. The air was pollen-thick. With his back spiked into the makeshift wall of hay, Eddie felt his city nose begin to run. He heard the scratch and crackle of tiny stones under Mikey's boots as he moved inside. He stood up.

'Who's there?' Mikey said, his voice rising. 'Come out. I've got a gun.'

'You don't need a gun, Mikey. It's me.' Eddie stood on the yellow edge of light, scraps of hay falling from his shoulders, the lantern blasting them white as they fell. He wondered whether he was about to go the way of Rory, right here, on the cold floor.

Mikey's head jerked up as if he'd taken an uppercut straight on the chin. His mouth opened, wide as a scream, a thin whale-song howl shooting into the eaves. He threw the gun high and left. They watched it together, the arc of it, heard the thudding sound as it landed on a great roll of tarpaulin. For a moment they both stared at the butt of the shotgun, its barrel pointing back towards the house. Mikey was swaying on his feet. Eddie thought he was going to collapse but with a roar he ran straight at him. They fell together, Mikey rolling him hard across the floor, strong as a bear.

'What the fuck, Eddie! Goddamn it. What the fuck are you doing here?'

Eddie was no match for a man who'd been farming since he was twelve. And he'd been wrong about Mikey. What he lacked in height he made up for in breadth. He smelled of diesel and coffee and, surprisingly, good soap. Eddie waited for the fist. Knew it would be bad.

But in the heaving roll, Mikey's curses hot on his face, the starburst of pain did not come. Prising away a shoulder, heavy as a stone, Eddie got to his feet and shook

181

himself down. Mikey drew huge breaths from the green-tanged floor.

'You have no right,' Mikey said, breathing hard. 'You have no right to come here.' His voice was choking.

Eddie knew he was crying. He walked to the tarpaulin, stared down at the gun as if he'd never seen one before. 'I know,' he said. 'But I had to come.'

Mikey wiped his shirt-sleeve roughly across his face, looked up at Eddie with a disbelieving stare. 'In the barn, Eddie.' He shook his head. 'What sort of sick joke is this?'

Eddie looked into the corner where everything had ended. 'You didn't burn it down, Mikey.' He couldn't help himself. 'Your dad said he'd burn it down. After Rory.'

Eddie had slept in cars before, when there was nowhere else to go. The nights here came down so black and quiet, colder than he'd expected. This was the second night, up by the front gate, the farmhouse shuttered against him, the rise of the land tipping him towards the road at a slight angle.

Mikey would not speak to him tonight either, Eddie had decided. Not this late. His shoulder still ached, and there was a long bruise forming on his shin. He was pulling up the old travel rug, still amazed that he'd thought to bring it. When he looked again at the house, Mikey was standing beneath the light over the front door, a corona of small insects playing around his head.

Eddie got out of the car slowly, his leg complaining, and walked the few steps to the fence. He was relieved to see there was no sign of the shotgun. Mikey would not, Eddie knew, be a knife man.

'Listen, Mikey ...' Eddie called across to him. He heard the trembling whinny of a screech owl. 'I know this is going to seem really strange, but I need to talk to you about a painting.' Something slithered close to Eddie's foot and shot away. He had a sudden longing for asphalt.

Mikey didn't speak. He just stared back down the steps, out into the darkness.

'Mikey, I need to come in. Please. I need to tell you about ...' Eddie cast his head left and right, wondering where to begin.

'I know about the painting,' Mikey said.

It had been over thirty years, but his aunt and uncle's old place looked much the same. The long narrow hall. The lurid wallpaper with the fat stripes that Mikey's father, whisky-crazy one Christmas, had tried to rip from the walls. The house felt brighter, somehow. Cleaner. The kitchen had been redone. But there were no small touches. It was a big square room looking out across the farm. The barn loomed in the moonlight, its edges white as bones.

There were no curtains. The benchtops were bare. Eddie suspected that the cupboards were, too. Hunkered in one corner, a green enamel stove looked shiny and barely used. There's no woman, Eddie thought. He savoured the idea of Mikey alone like a lozenge in his mouth.

Mikey motioned to him to sit at the kitchen table.

Eddie sat with his back to the barn, feeling its presence push against his shoulders. He saw that the old coffee pot was still in use. Mikey put a plate of cold food on the table in front of him. Sliced meats, some fine-looking cheese. He cut a thick hunk of bread with his mother's bone-handled knife and put it on Eddie's plate. The coffee smelled good.

'Mikey, I'm sorry about the way I turned up.' Eddie felt light-headed. Days and nights in the car. He thought of the painting and nothing seemed real. He wondered about Rory. Was he really dead? He picked at a corner of the bread crust. 'It was just that when I got here and saw the place and ...'

Eddie wanted to say that when that last hill dropped away he'd thought maybe there'd be a rough scar where the old barn had been, maybe even a new barn straddling all that pain, but when he saw the red roof of it, the white walls newly painted, and a tree, a fucking dogwood on one corner, everything neat and solid and alive, he could have put a hole in Mikey that moment, as easy as look at him. And feeling that hate surge through him, he almost turned back for Brooklyn to be scared of a dead boy staring out of an ancient picture, because that was better than this.

But he didn't say any of these things. He took a slice of meat, made a roll of it with his fingers and said, 'I didn't mean to be in the barn. I really didn't.'

Mikey pushed a coffee cup towards Eddie. He seemed in no mood to sit down. 'Judy's away. She's at her mother's while I paint the inside here.' Then he gestured to the food in front of Eddie. 'That's the best I can do for you tonight.'

Eddie felt the meat lump in his mouth. He took a sip of hot coffee. He wasn't sure how much time Mikey was going to give him. 'You said you know about the painting.'

Mikey hesitated, then reached across the kitchen bench behind him and picked up a large envelope. From it, he pulled out a smaller envelope and handed it to Eddie without a word.

In one of its linen-textured corners, Eddie could trace the embossed outline of a cone-shaped tree. It was addressed to his mother. Feeling suddenly cold, he put it down on the table between them.

'Open it,' Mikey said.

The envelope was lined. White on brilliant white. Inside was a plain, folded card, handwritten, the inked curves shaky in parts.

Dear Mrs Reynolds,

I did not wish to appear rude yesterday and if that is how it seemed, then I apologise. I am sorry to hear of your health issues. The trials of an illness can make one impatient and ill-suited to even the most prosaic of matters. Please believe me when I say that I understand this better than you can know.

The situation that you outlined to me is far from pedestrian. I can well understand your feelings of distress. Regrettably, I must reiterate that I cannot help you in any way with regard to the painting. It is not unknown for people to believe that a work of art can have powers beyond what is depicted on the canvas. I admit that I would have once scoffed at such a suggestion. However, quite early in my career I encountered a painting that I came to believe had some sort of malign force. It is not easy for me to forget the turmoil that picture seemed to engender.

I have written more than I intended. The painting you have is undoubtedly valuable. Selling it would solve some of your problems, but perhaps not all. I can only add that the painting that I encountered years ago was later burned by its owners, a step they did not regret.

Sincerely,
Walter Fennell

Eddie felt a pounding in his head. His skull felt heavy enough to tip him, face first, onto the lino floor. He almost wished for its cool flatness against his cheek.

His mother. Walter. Mikey.

'Where did you get this letter?' he said to Mikey.

'Aunt Anne sent it. A few months before she died.' Mikey paused, made a half-turn away. 'That, and a few other things.'

'What other things?'

Mikey hesitated. 'There was a letter for me.'

Eddie almost snorted. 'To you? You're telling me my mother wrote to you.'

Mikey, who had a powerful taste for silence, took a seat at the table. Eddie pushed his food around the plate, feeling Mikey's stare on his bent head.

'I didn't mean it like that,' Eddie mumbled. He would have liked a drink. 'Can I see my mother's letter?'

'No. She asked me to destroy it afterwards, and I did,' Mikey said. 'You'll just have to believe me.'

'So now you're going to tell me that my mother forgave you for shooting her favourite son.' Eddie could hear his own belligerent tone. He half expected a blow before he'd finished the sentence.

But Mikey's patience was prodigious. He looked out towards the barn. 'In her own way,' he said, 'I guess she did.' He poured himself some coffee, pointedly ignoring Eddie's drained cup. 'Look, Eddie, I can't make much sense of all this, but here's what I understand: the painting seems to be haunted in some way.'

'No!' Eddie stood up with a harsh scrape of chair. He would not let Mikey say this. Mikey was a farmer. Used to ordinary things. Used to weather and soil and animals. Hearing Mikey, seeing Walter's words on the card – pursed-lipped Walter – was too much. 'I can't believe you're coming out with this stuff, Mikey. This is just crap.' He felt the need to run from the room.

'Sit down!' Mikey's voice was loud in the empty kitchen. 'Listen to me, Eddie. You're the one who drove all the way to Ohio with your hair standing on end. You're the one I found hanging around the barn like some sort of freak.

You're the one who sat outside my house for two nights freezing your nuts off, so don't tell me I'm talking crap. You know I'm not.'

Eddie sat. Mikey reached back, picked up the larger envelope, held it up, his face red. 'Your mother wrote to me because she wanted to finish things.' Mikey tapped angrily on Walter's card. 'She sent me this letter from some gallery in Brooklyn that says weird shit does happen and' – he shook the envelope in his hand – 'she wrote the saddest letter I ever … one that … will stay with me …'

Eddie saw the words catch in Mikey's throat. The cousins stared at each other across the table. He wants me to go, Eddie thought.

'She kept dreaming about the painting,' Mikey went on. 'Your mother. She kept it wrapped up, hidden away in a cupboard. That's what she told me. She couldn't understand about the dreams, so she took it out one day. When she looked at it, she reckoned she could see her Uncle Ivan in the painting. She swore he wasn't there before. Do you remember that uncle who got some rare medal in the war?'

Eddie felt a sting of shame. 'Yeah. Heard of him,' he said. 'How did she even know what he looked like?'

Mikey tipped up the large envelope. A small photo slid out onto the table. An old photo of a young soldier. A doomed boy on his doomed horse. Eddie picked it up. On the back, in faded ink: *Ivan on Jasper. 1917.*

'She went to see this Fennell guy,' Mikey said, 'to try and get rid of the picture. Sell it, or whatever. He wouldn't touch it, and she didn't have the courage to burn it. In the end' – Mikey wouldn't meet Eddie's eye – 'she left it for you.'

Eddie stared. There was a soft click in his brain. 'She left it for me. So that I'd break the spell. Sell it for drink money or something.' The shame rose hotly up his neck.

Mikey ignored him. 'After her Uncle Ivan appeared,' he said, 'she was even more terrified of that damn painting. She believed – her whole family believed, from way back – that when a new figure appeared, the next one had been chosen.'

'Mikey, what are you talking about?'

'That's what she told me, Eddie,' Mikey said. 'Once her Uncle Ivan appeared, she knew the next one had been chosen. She was sure it would be Rory.'

Eddie felt the barn like a shadow on his back. He was tired beyond measure.

'It was Rory,' Eddie said.

1827. Bear Park Field, Shadwell, East London.

'You're afraid of water, aren't you?' he said.

They were taking the longer way this time, now that he was so much stronger.

'Yes,' Thomas said. 'I nearly drowned when I was a boy.'

'In the pond?'

'Yes.'

The field was almost empty. No one could hear them talking.

'Yet you still went in to pull me out.'

Thomas smiled. 'Yes, I did.'

The evenings were brighter now, the ground dry again.

'Thomas, I shall be leaving tomorrow.'

'Oh.' Thomas was surprised. Disappointed. 'Where will you go?'

'Somewhere you won't follow, my friend,' he said with a smile, taking Thomas' arm. 'Across the sea.'

Thomas knew he would not be any more specific.

'But I have a gift for you. To thank you for saving my life.'

'How very kind,' said Thomas. He could not remember the last time anyone had given him anything.

'It's a painting,' he said. 'To honour your courage.'

His English has really improved, Thomas thought. 'Oh dear, that's far too grand for me,' Thomas said, laughing. They wheeled back towards Fox Lane. Susannah would be waiting.

'It isn't grand at all, dear friend,' he told Thomas. 'It's just a small, square painting. But I will make sure that you are not forgotten. That I promise you.'

Eddie watched the rental car being driven back to its bay. Mink-coloured mud fanned up its flanks in the shape of small wings, but there was not another mark on it. He had tried not to look too astonished when the young woman had said it was, 'Fine, just fine, thank you, sir.'

He tried to get a clear vision of the journey back to Brooklyn but it would not come. He'd eaten somewhere. A vague memory of tuna sandwiches. Rain. Miles out, the car had meandered across the centre line before veering back, a blast of truck horn roaring across the hood.

'Don't you see?' Mikey had said to him. 'You're related – we're related – to everyone in the painting. Ivan,

Rory, everyone else. Although God knows who they all are. Aunt Anne wrote down as much as she knew.'

It would be a long walk back to the apartment from the rental place. Eddie wanted to get home, he wanted to see the painting, but he couldn't resist a detour. The place was less than two hundred yards off to the left now. The wind cut at his ribs as soon as he turned into the side road, but he needed to have a look. It was closed, of course, at this hour, the day's discarded packaging twisting up the thin stairway.

At the glass door, Eddie looked in. The pictures were shadowy but visible. Everything seemed the same. He stood in the semi-darkness, under a row of halogen lights. The tattoo parlour nearby was still open. He could hear music coming from inside, although there was no one around. He thought of his mother coming here, a broken woman making her way up these stairs, carrying a painting she feared. In his own stilted way, Eddie thought, Walter had tried to help her. Burn it, he'd all but said. For the first time, Eddie felt glad that the painting had survived.

He cupped his hands on the glass, and squinted into the gallery. He saw that the little tree was gone.

He's sick, Eddie thought. He was sure now. He remembered the minuscule shake in Walter's head, the pronounced tremble in his hand. Eddie was surprised to find that he felt genuinely sorry. Turning to go, he noticed a small typewritten card mounted on the glass: *Fennell Gallery is closed until further notice.*

He probably lives near here, Eddie thought. He looked along the countless windows banked above the street. Any one of them could be his. It would be tasteful inside, Eddie imagined. Walter's favourite pieces would be framed and hung, just so. It would be immaculately clean. Nothing out of place. And at its heart, Eddie felt sure, a man would be dying, stylishly, hopelessly alone.

Eddie waited for a moment, the cold threading around him in the narrow entrance. He thought of Walter's note to his mother, the oddly confidential tone. He thought of the scratch of Walter's fountain pen, the erratic slips in the ink, evident even then. Tiny lightning bolts of ruin.

Eddie watched the litter crackle and skitter around his feet, tumbling into the corners. Suddenly affronted, he reached down, scooped it all up, and stuffed it deep into his pocket.

On the walk from Walter's place, Eddie imagines another man coming home, a world away, centuries away. A man with a Reynolds nose.

The man sees a body, face down in the local pond. Mortally afraid, he drags it to the side, peeling away the drown-heavy coat, spotting a tremble of life in the sodden chest. Somehow, he gets the man home, in by the fire, harries his wife for clothes and blankets. Two days later, eyelids flutter open. The man cannot speak English. He cannot, or will not, give his name. He has, it turns out, an uncommon dexterity in his hands. As his chest recovers, he helps Thomas with the keys and locks that he sells in the markets and street corners. He teaches Thomas a way with a tumbling mechanism that would keep the Reynolds family comfortable for the rest of their lives.

During the day, while Thomas is still at work, the man paints. Thomas' wife resents the cost of the oils. 'Leave him be, Susannah,' Thomas tells her. She gets used to the man's strange but unobtrusive ways. Before he disappears forever, he presents the couple with a magnificent rendition of their street, framed in black wood, thick as a child's arm. Every stone, every wall, the sheen of the apples, the drain of foul water at the road's edge is perfect.

'But it's empty,' Susannah says to her husband. 'Where are all the people?'

'They will come later,' the man says.

Susannah is stunned to find he can speak English. Thomas has known for some time.

On the roadside, before he leaves, he talks quietly to Thomas. 'You will appear in the painting after your death. Don't be afraid about this, my friend. It will not hasten your end in any way, although foolish people will tell themselves that it does, and grow fearful of it.'

Thomas assures him that he is not afraid.

'There will be others,' the man says. 'The best of those who come after you. The ones who are like you.' He shakes Thomas' hand solemnly, and is gone.

Thomas Reynolds does not mention this to Susannah, for fear that she might think it the Devil's work and put the painting in the fire. He keeps it wrapped, telling her he is afraid of smoke damage, hoping she'll forget its empty street.

Thomas lives a long life, well beyond Susannah. When their son finds the hidden painting he takes it with him to America, puts it on his wall, and marvels at the portrait of his father with his bundles of keys as big as cabbage heads.

Not cursed. Haunted. That's what Mikey had told him. 'Some things we just have to accept, Eddie.' And Eddie knew what he meant.

As he had driven away from the farm, he'd seen again the dogwood tree that Mikey had planted for Rory, its red buds heavy and beautiful, lifted up for the birds to come, to strip it down, to be bare and ready once more.

Brooklyn's streets were cold. When Eddie pushed at the main door, he felt the full weight of his fatigue. As he took the last of the stairs up to his apartment, his mind ran with faces and roads. The uncertain voice of the screech owl, its lonely, tremulous cry. The sense of things shifting and settling.

There was a note stuck in the jamb of the door: *Where are you? Give me a ring. Frank. PS: Grew up in Alaska, if you must know.*

Eddie was not afraid, not like before. But his heart still knocked loud in his chest. He turned into the main room.

'Hello, Rory,' he said, going in.

He sat down.

Acknowledgements

Encouragement. It seems to me that this is one of the finest gifts a writer can receive. A great deal of it has come my way: from my extended family, from friends, from other writers. I acknowledge, with sincere thanks, every single time someone has asked how my writing is going, and cared about the answer. I thank those who have read early drafts of my stories, who have given of their time and expertise to provide valuable feedback, who have celebrated when publication and awards came, and commiserated when they did not. I dedicate this book to my husband, Adrian – always my first and best reader – and to our son, Louis, who spent his teenage years listening to my stories, and encouraging me to write some happier ones!

In 2016, I was honoured to receive a Queensland Writers Fellowship. Through this wonderful award, which brought financial and professional encouragement, I was fortunate enough to be mentored by Judith Lukin-Amundsen. Her assistance and support were invaluable to me. Thank you to my publisher, UQP: to Madonna Duffy, for believing in my work, and to Aviva Tuffield and her team, including Felicity Dunning and Jean Smith, for shaping and guiding my collection.

I am deeply indebted to many who have supported my writing in diverse ways, including Ruth Blair, Kate Eltham, Karen Hollands, Ann Hughes, Kay Kelly, Mary McHugh, Steve Plowman, Felicity Plunkett, Fiona Robertson, Jude Seaboyer, Chris Tiffin and Rita Tynan. I honour the memory of David Nokes, a fine teacher and writer at King's College London, who encouraged me to publish my stories. Ronnie O'Callaghan, my 'Irish agent', did not live to see this book come to fruition but his uplifting support has not been forgotten. There are many others, too numerous to mention here, whose practical, professional and emotional support has meant so much to me. Thank you.

Versions of the following stories have appeared online and in print. Thank you to the editors of these publications and the conveners of these literary awards.

'A Widow's Snow', *Review of Australian Fiction*, Volume 10, Issue 1, 2014.

'An Uncommon Occurrence', Allingham Festival Flash Fiction Competition, 2015.

'The Turn', Carmel Bird Award for New Crime Writing, 2015; and *Crime Scenes: Stories*, ed. Zane Lovitt, Spineless Wonders, 2016.

'The News', *Things Left and Found by the Side of the Road*, Bath Flash Fiction, Volume 3, 2018.

'Things', *Bristol Short Story Prize Anthology*, Tangent Books, Volume 10, 2017.

'The Mohair Coat', Flash500 Flash Fiction Competition, 2016.

'Legacy', *Review of Australian Fiction*, Volume 5, Issue 5, 2013.

'Thirty Years', *Flash: The International Short-Short Story Magazine*, Volume 11.1, 2019.

'Cutting the Cord', InkTears Flash Fiction Awards, 2016.

'The Golden Hour', published as 'When the Pitch Drops', Flash500 Annual Short Story Contest, 2018.

'Death of a Friend', *Ripening: National Flash-Fiction Day Anthology*, 2018.

'Tying the Boats', Bath Flash Fiction Award, 2017; and *The Lobsters Run Free*, Bath Flash Fiction, Volume 2, 2017.

'The Memory Bones', *Amanda Lohrey Selects*, Spineless Wonders, 2012.

'The Way It Sounds', *Things Left and Found by the Side of the Road*, Bath Flash Fiction, Volume 3, 2018.

'The Painting', Aeon Award, 2013; and *Albedo One Magazine*, Issue 47, 2016.

Also in UQP's short fiction series

TRICK OF THE LIGHT
Laura Elvery

Shortlisted, Queensland Literary Awards
University of Southern Queensland Short Story
Collection – Steele Rudd Award 2018

With a keen eye for detail and rich emotional insight, Laura Elvery reveals the fears and fantasies of everyday people searching for meaning. Ranging from tender poignancy to wry humour, *Trick of the Light* is the beguiling debut collection from one of Australia's rising stars.

'Radiant, accomplished and exquisitely written, this is an outstanding collection.' Ryan O'Neill

'*Trick of the Light* is at times haunting and poetic, other times bright and sharp, and always memorable and hopeful … This thoroughly profound, bold and playful debut pulled me along and pulled me apart.' Brooke Davis

ISBN 978 0 7022 6006 3

UQP